CHRISTOPHER AND THE QUASI-WAR WITH FRANCE

Published by The Nautical & Aviation Publishing Company of America, Inc.
1250 Fairmont Avenue, Mount Pleasant, South Carolina 29464.

Library of Congress Catalog Card Number: 2002029528

ISBN: 1-877853-65-8

Printed in the United States of America

Library of Congress Cataloging-in-Publication Data

Mack, William P., 1915.
        Christopher and the quasi war with France/by William P.
        Mack. p. cm.
        ISBN 1-877853-65-8
        1. United States–History–1794-1801–Fiction. 2. United
        States–Foreign relations–France– Fiction.   3. France–
        Foreign relations–United States–Fiction. 4. Shipbuilding
        industry– Fiction. 5. Annapolis (Md.)–Fiction. I. Title.

        PS3563.A3132C492002
        813'.54–dc21   2002029528

CHRISTOPHER AND THE QUASI-WAR WITH FRANCE

a novel of the sea

by

WILLIAM P. MACK

The Nautical & Aviation Publishing Company of America
Charleston, South Carolina

Chapter 1

The merchant ship *Arundel,* three weeks sailing from her home port of Annapolis, had left Athens five days ago the first of March, 1794. Her hold was filled with carefully wrapped greek pottery and dishware. The owners, a group of Annapolis merchants, had agreed with her captain to load the after hold to capacity with valuable but light cargo. The forward hold had been converted to berthing for twenty extra hands. Gunpowder had been placed in a magazine, and a hundred 12-pound balls had been arranged in racks around the bulwarks. The extra hands were to man twelve 12-pounders placed at the bow chaser and stern positions and along the sides of the ship. Because she had been constructed to serve either as a merchant ship or as a privateer, she had eight gun ports on each side, which could be used quickly to fire from either side.

The *Arundel* had been built at the Christopher Shipyard in Annapolis. Her captain, Artemis Arnold, had agreed to assume command if young Christopher, who had helped design and construct her, would join her crew, so John Paul Christopher was serving as second officer.

Captain Arnold hoped to coax an additional knot or two out of the already fast schooner-rigged ship. Actually she was now making about two extra knots using a ballast plan devised by Christopher and some rigging and sail modifications made to her by Christopher. He was now standing the watch, and the last log cast had shown eleven knots. The fifteen knot wind astern was speeding them toward the Straits of Gibraltar, some five hundred miles ahead.

Captain Arnold walked over to the binnacle, glanced at the wake aft, and instructed the young helmsman, "Mind your helm, lad. The straighter you steer the faster we'll go. That lessens our chances of being caught by Algerian pirates."

The sailor shuddered. "The pilot in Athens told me that the Algerian prisons are the worst in the world."

"That's right," agreed the captain.

The helmsman said, "Then we were lucky to make the passage east without seeing any pirate ships."

The captain pulled a chart of the Mediterranean from the binnacle and studied it carefully as Christopher looked over his shoulder. Captain Arnold ran his finger along the projected course of the ship, and said, "I make it forty-eight hours to Gibraltar. This will put us off Oran tommorow at dawn and could cause trouble."

Christopher examined the chart. "The Mediterranean narrows to a hundred miles off Oran and doesn't get any better."

The captain nodded. "We'll have to enter that area at dawn, and if we make it through, we'll pass Gibraltar by dawn the next day."

"Did the Consul at Athens know anything about the Algerians and the pirates based there?" asked Christopher.

The captain rubbed his full mustache and took a deep breath into his barrel chest. "It's bad news. They captured eight American merchant ships in the last two months."

The first officer came on deck, stretching his arms. "I heard what you two were talking about. I hope you'll get some sleep, Christopher, because you'll be taking over the watch at midnight. I'm guessing we'll see pirates at first light."

MacGowan, was about fifty years old, and a long and hard life at sea had left its marks on his bronzed skin, now covered with wrinkles centered about his eyes. MacGowan, the Gunner, and the Boatswain were all old men. They and the captain were being well paid and had all been lured out of retirement by the Annapolis merchants. The extra sailors had been similarly recruited and were aching to see some action and a promised bonus. The officers had seen more than their share of action, except for young Christopher, and all hoped to return home without encountering any pirates.

Before he went below, Christopher looked carefully at the sails and rigging. "Captain, I suggest we ease the pressure on the sails. Unlike other ships she moves faster with a little slack in the middle of her sails."

The captain nodded. "Very well. MacGowan, make it so."

The ship was schooner-rigged using two large masts. Each mast supported a large sail flowing aft and two jibs to the bowsprit. Trisails could be rigged above the large sails but were seldom used. Without them, two men could handle the sails of each mast, whereas a two masted square-rigged ship needed at least ten men per watch. Now the wind was almost dead astern, and both sails were about ninety degrees out to starboard. If desired, one sail could be shifted to the other side, allowing the ship to sail "wing and wing". Since the forward sail would then have its own direct wind, another knot was possible, but the captain chose to use the present rig in order to remain as maneuverable as possible. "It's worth the other knot," he had said.

Christopher listened to the sounds of the wind passing by the sails and rigging. The sails were held to the masts by large wooden rings, and when they were trimmed tightly, the rings did not slap against the masts. But when they were rigged like Christopher wanted them, an occasional slap could be heard. Now he heard one and was content. It was music to him. The sounds of the wind vibrating in the standing rigging produced notes that indicated it was tight enough to keep the masts in proper alignment.

He admired the deep blue of the Mediterranean water, slightly bluer than they would soon find in the Atlantic. Also the waves were shorter and smaller. A group of flying fish rose and glided along for a hundred yards before plopping back into the water. Christopher sighed. He loved the ocean, but right now it was threatening and he knew he needed rest.

Christopher slept soundly until midnight and then took over the watch until 4 a.m. When he was relieved, he went below but could not sleep. At 5 a.m. he rolled carefully out of his heaving cot and dressed. He then went back on deck.

MacGowan laughed. "You're here early. It isn't even dawn yet."

Christopher took a deep breath and scannned the horizon. "Yes, but it will be in a few minutes."

Christopher went over to MacGowan, who was standing by the binnacle to check the young helmsman's ability to steer a straight course. "He's all right," MacGowan concluded. "Now I can enjoy watching the ship sail for a few minutes before all hell breaks loose."

The two walked aft and leaned on the bulwark. "Listen to that," MacGowan said. "Waves slapping under the counter."

Young Christopher smiled. "Yes, and the wind would also be singing through the rigging, but it's only fifteen knots from astern and we're making eleven."

MacGowan looked forward at the beautiful lines of the ship. "She's very graceful. Turns easily like a dancer. Sails fast, and still carries a lot of cargo. Look at her condition. The extra men have been cleaning and polishing like mad. We have more men than we need for daily work, but I keep them all busy."

"She's well designed," added Christopher, but her successors will be twice as big. The French are designing larger and faster ships, and we'll be fighting against them for years."

MacGowan scratched his bushy head. "By the way, what is this Quasi-war you keep talking about?"

Christopher laughed. "It means resembling but not actual. Neither war nor peace, but both at once. We will not declare war on France, neither will they on us, but we're going to be fighting each other for years, sinking and capturing each other's ships."

MacGowan sighed. "Sounds like war to me."

Then Christopher sighed. "It won't be very good for our country, but on the other hand it will be fine for my family."

"I don't understand."

"Our family shipyard and business are almost bankrupt."

"Will the war help?" asked MacGowan.

"I hope so, and we want to fight. We expect to build several larger versions of both the privateers and the merchant forms of this ship and sell them for profit. My father expects to take at least one of the privateer versions to sea and capture some French merchantmen. The cargos they bring back from the Caribbean are very valuable, or they will be as soon as the law is changed to permit us to keep the reward."

"Will you be going to sea with your father?"

"I don't think so. He wants me to stay at the shipyard, designing and building ships. He'll find someone else to go to sea with him."

MacGowan stretched and yawned. "If he needs someone, I'm available."

Just before 6 a.m. a faint light began to break through the clouds, but with the hazy weather it was still mostly dark. The light, coming from the east, reflected off two small white spots ahead, one to the right of their course and another to their left.

"Damn!" Christopher shouted as he pounded the bulwark. "There they are." He turned to MacGowan and said, "you'd better call the captain."

"He'll be here any moment," MacGowan replied. "He can smell dawn and trouble."

Within minutes the captain came on deck, carrying a mug of coffee.

"There are two bastards out there," MacGowan said.

The captain nodded. "We are lucky there aren't more. Change course to the northwest."

"Are you going to try to pass them to the north?"

MacGowan asked, "No. I just want them to think we are," replied Captain Arnold. "Rouse the crew and shift the other four broadside guns to the starboard side."

The gunner, a grizzled black man, came on deck. He had been a master gunner in a British frigate and had been lured back to sea by the promise of a very large bonus.

The pirate to the north changed course to the northeast, obviously to meet the *Arundel*. The ship to the south was too far away to be a factor at present, but Christopher made a mental note to keep track of her.

As the full light spread and the two ships closed, the captain pulled a long glass from the binnacle cabinet and climbed lightly up the port ratlines. He examined the pirate for a full five minutes before coming down.

"Well?" MacGowan asked.

Arnold explained, "She's a sister ship to this one. She must have been captured during the last two months."

"How does she look?" asked MacGowan.

"Awful. The rigging is slack and the sails are ill-kept. Even though she's a sister ship, we'll outsail her by three knots."

"How does the crew look?"

The captain laughed. "The crew looks like a bunch of pirates, dressed in flowing rags, each armed with a fancy sword. The captain is waving around a six foot curved scimitar that he can hardly lift."

Christopher took a deep breath. "I still don't want to board them. What will we do? We're heading for a meeting."

The captain laughed. "Not for long." He turned to MacGowan, "I know the guns will be firing to starboard soon, but line up the crew along the port bulwark so the pirates will think we'll be firing to port. Open the gun ports on both sides."

Five minutes later MacGowan came aft. "We're ready, Captain."

The captain turned to the gunner, "Gunner, let me know when we reach maximum range."

The gunner grinned. "I can hardly wait."

The group on the quarterdeck waited tensely as the range decreased.

Then the gunner raised his hand. "Now, Captain."

The captain took a deep breath and shouted, "Wear ship! Left full helm! Commence firing!"

The ship swung rapidly to port. The gunner ordered the bow chasers to fire, and as soon as the broadside guns could bear, he ordered them to fire from forward so the smoke would clear from the other guns.

As the ship swung to the southwest the captain ordered, "Steady on southwest." He turned to watch the fall of shot. "Damn, Gunner, you were perfect. All but one ball landed on their deck or damaged their sails. Now give them our stern chasers and try to get another salvo ready."

The last two guns boomed out, but the projectiles fell short because of the opening range.

In the meantime, most of the shots from the pirate fell a few yards short, except for one that came in through the after gun port. It shoved the gun across the deck and smashed the wooden gun carriage. The gun crushed a man against the opposite bulwark and two other men fell after being hit by pieces of the flying carriage. MacGowan ran forward to tend to them, but the captain stayed aft. He had seen Christopher fall when a piece of the gun carriage had swept his legs out from under him. He ran to Christopher and turned him over. "Are you all right?" he asked.

Christopher moaned, "My left leg. It hurts."

Then Captain Arnold looked at Christopher's leg and felt it gingerly. When the Captain probed halfway up the calf, Christopher moaned. "That's it," he said.

The Captain pulled out his knife and slit the trouser leg

up to the knee. He examined the left calf tenderly.

"It's broken," he concluded. "This is a green stick fracture, meaning the ends are still together. I'll be able to set it and make a splint out of swab handles. Just lie there while I get the ship out of danger."

The captain ran back to the quarterdeck and glanced at the two pirate ships.

MacGowan said, "The first ship won't be able to catch us. He's more than a gunshot behind us and is falling further behind. The other ship turned earlier to the west trying to intercept us." The captain watched the laboring pirate for a few minutes. Then he ordered, "Shift the guns to port. Move the dead and wounded aft. Leave young Christopher alone. He'll be all right where he is. I'll take care of him as soon as I can."

The second pirate closed quickly. The captain said, "If I change course to the north, the first pirate will catch up with us. Gunner, commence firing when the southern pirate is in range."

When the gunner indicated they were in range, the captain ordered, "Come left to open the battery." The ship swung rapidly to port and Captain Arnold shouted, "Commence firing!"

The pirate decided to hold course and use her bow chasers, but they fell short. At the same time, the *Arundel's* salvo landed on the pirate's forecastle. Pieces of gun carriages flew in all directions.

The captain shouted, "Good work, Gunner. You fixed him right! Now he'll have to turn away to open his broadside."

The pirate got off a salvo at long range, and one ball landed aboard, tearing up the bulwark and skidding across the ship without touching anything. Then it bounced over the side.

"Damn!" MacGowan shouted. "We got out of that with only a couple of gouges in our deck."

The pirate began to fall behind, and her salvos landed

well astern.

The Captain shouted, "We've made it! Come back to the west."

MacGowan let out his breath. "Now all we have to do is make the strait."

"You're right. Now tend to the wounded. I'll take care of Christopher."

Captain Arnold walked over to Christopher, now being tended by captain's steward. "How is he?" the captain asked.

"He hurts, but it's getting better," answered the steward.

"Go back to my cabin and get a bottle of laudanum. Then go to the boatswain and ask him to give you four three - foot lengths of swab handle and two extra swabs."

When the steward returned, the captain bent over Christopher. "This is laudanum. Take a good swig, and let me know when the pain subsides."

In ten minutes Christopher sighed. "Go ahead," he said weakly.

The captain and the steward held Christopher's upper body steady, and then the captain steadily pulled on his ankle. When the leg was straight, he placed the four pieces of swab handle around the leg and had the steward hold them in place while he wrapped them with pieces of oakum. The captain and steward pulled Christopher up on his feet. He staggered briefly and then said, "I'll be all right. The laudanum is making me dizzy."

When he was safely in his cot, he said, "I'll be all right in a few hours. The boatswain can take my watch, but I want to be on deck tomorrow morning to command my gun battery. Just lend me one of your chairs."

The captain laughed. "I know you will want to, and I need you. Steward, bring him up on deck at 3 a.m."

———◦———

The ship flew westward with the captain trying to squeeze every knot he could out of the ship. Darkness came without further sightings. The captain said to MacGowan, "They'll all be off Oran, or one or two will be in the straits of Gibraltar."

At first light Captain Arnold, MacGowan, and Christopher perched in a chair, stood on the quarterdeck scanning the horizon when the dawn began to break. Their first discernible image was the monstrous black head of Gibraltar. A few small points of light along the top twinkled, and then a cluster of lights came in to view from the harbor at its foot. Then the black turned to gray.

The captain pulled out his chart. "We're still ten miles from the entrance. We'll find them at the southern side. That's close to home for them, and the Moroccans won't bother them."

The light continued to grow. Then they simultaneously sighted a faint glow of white sail near the southern arm of land at the entrance.

"There's one!" shouted the captain. "Call the crew to battle stations and man the guns to port."

When the daylight was full, they could see the pirate ship steering toward them. "Ha!" the captain said. "He thinks he's about to take an innocent merchantman." Captain Arnold ordered the gunner, to lift all the gun ports and run the guns out."

The two ships neared each other. At a thousand yards the captain could see that the pirate ship was smaller than they were. "They've sent a boy to do a man's job," he said. "Come two points to starboard so our batteries will bear."

When the gunner decided they were in range, the captain shouted, "Commence firing!"

The first shots hit, and a scattered salvo came back. The captain scrutinized the pirate ship through his long glass. Then he laughed. "She's decided we're too much for her. She's turning away."

MacGowan looked puzzled. "What is she doing? We only fired one salvo."

"Our firing caused a lot of damage. I can see dead and

wounded about the decks."

"Are they going to change course and run away to the south?" MacGowan asked.

"I think they'd like to, but they've given up. Two long boats are being lowered, and the crew is swarming over each other to get into them." The captain ordered, "Cease fire! Close the ship."

When they were alongside the captain said, "Lower the sails and put a boat in the water."

MacGowan looked puzzled. "Are you going to board her?"

"Certainly. By the time our party gets there they'll all be rowing ashore to Morocco. The beach is not far from them." The Captain then ordered, "Gunner, take five men and board her. See if she has anything of use and if so, bring it back."

"Aye aye, sir."

"And when you've done that, open her seacocks, set a powder train to her magazines, and abandon her in a hurry."

The boat was rowed rapidly away, and those on the quarterdeck could see the party scrambling aboard and then going below. A whisp of black smoke came up. "He's lit the powder train," the captain said. "Raise our sails and move away before she blows. The gunner can catch us."

In a few minutes the party scrambled back over the side and rowed rapidly after the *Arundel* as she moved away.

The gunner came aboard and directed that the boat be hoisted. The black whisp became a cloud and then the ship erupted. The gunner squinted. "I don't know whether the seacocks or the magazine got her first. She is a smelly crate and deserves to be sunk."

The captain asked, "Gunner, what did you bring back?"

The gunner shook his head. "There wasn't much there, sir. I think we were supposed to be their first victim. There are a dozen fancy swords in the bottom of the boat. I brought you the captain's scimitar."

"Thank you, Gunner. After you've selected your own,

let the officers and crew draw lots for the others."

They watched as the ship sank in a cloud of black smoke and steam. Behind them the two boats of pirates landed on the shore, and the crews staggered up the rocky beach.

"That's it," the captain said. "Set course for the Chesapeake Bay entrance."

Chapter 2

On a muggy day in July 1794, a little over two months after the *Arundel* had returned to port, the men of the Christopher family sat around an open window in the spacious offices of the Christopher Shipbuilding Company overlooking Annapolis Harbor.

At 54, Eric Christopher was still a robust and handsome man, with a shock of receding white hair. He had retired from the shipyard a few years ago, following the Revolutionary War. Eric left his son Matthew in charge, and he now ran his second wife's horse farm outside of Annapolis. As a sideline, he raised a new breed of dog, now called the Chesapeake Bay Retriever. Two of them sat at his feet, panting slightly in the humid air.

Eric read from a Philadelphia paper, recently brought by the daily fast packet.

"Listen to this. The bad times in our business are over. President Washington has declared a three-month embargo against France and England as an economic reprisal for their actions against American shipping."

Matthew looked up. "What good does that do? Just words. What about the Algerian pirates?" At 35, Matthew was a younger version of his father, husky, handsome like his father, but with a full head of black hair, slightly gray, not receding. When he spoke, his teeth were white and regular. His face was covered with a stubble of recently shaved whiskers in the style of the day, and his nose was strong and almost prominent."

Matthew went on, "We are in a near crisis. We will have to close our business at the end of the year if we don't find some source of income."

Eric frowned. "You're right. Listen to this. This may be the means of our salvation. On 27 March 1794, the Congress passed an act to build four 44-gun frigates and

two of 36 guns. Then on the 28th, the Congress appointed captains and naval agents for the ships. Doesn't that
sound like business?"

"Yes, Father, but how will that help us? We can't build
ships that big."

Ryan Buchanan, the Irish-born foreman of the shipyard,
cleared his throat. He was regular featured and slim, but
strong. In a Maryland accent, slightly inflected with an Irish
brogue, he said, "Somebody has to build them. What does
the paper say?"

Eric turned to the next page. "Here it is. 'Joshua
Humphreys has been appointed the first builder of a frigate
and will be paid an annual salary of two-thousand dollars to
supervise the awarding of contracts and building of the
other ships.' The Congress really means business when it
spends its money that quickly."

Someone spoke up, "You mean our money."

Matthew laughed. "Mr. Humphreys is our 'in.' I know
him well and as you will remember I spent several months
working on the *Randolph*. While in his shipyard, I also
learned his techniques for building large ships."

Eric nodded. "You learned a lot that we used, but we
never got any contracts for the large ships built in those
days."

"We can use this knowledge," said Matthew. "There will
be an expanding market for ships, both for the Continental
Navy and for the merchantmen. The newer ships will have
to be a lot bigger than the ships we built during the
Revolutionary War."

Matthew's 20-year old son, John Paul Christopher,
named after Captain John Paul Jones, had been acting as
treasurer of the shipyard. He had brought his crutches from
the hospital, where he had gone to have his leg checked, and
was recovering rapidly. The hospital had declared the captain's leg setting well done. John Paul said, "We'll really
need some additional income. Our expenses have been con-
suming our capital for years."

John Paul had his mother's bearing and willowy physique rather than his father's stocky build. He was capable of spending long hours bent over his ledgers and still thinking clearly. After these tedious nights he frequently came up with innovations for accounting and even for shipbuilding. Now he was handicapped by his healing leg.

Eric Christopher nodded with grandfatherly pride. "He's right. Even my wife's horse farm is suffering, and I have drained from it all that I can. The only thing that has saved us are Matthew's wise investments from the prize money he made and our large profits from the shipyard during the war. But enough talk. Let's all get to work planning what to do with this new information. There should be some opportunities in it."

He got up, easing his arthritic joints, and whistled at the sleeping dogs. They came to and leaped up at him, eager to go outside. As Eric started to walk to the door, they ran outside and leaped into the back seat of the buggy Eric had specially built for his dogs. In it they could see forward and still not fall out of the seat.

Eric swore. "Look at that! The bitch stepped into a horse apple and spread it all over the back seat."

Matthew laughed. "What do you care? You used to say that the moment you got the rig back to the barn three men would be thoroughly cleaning it."

Eric frowned. "Yes, we used to have help, but my wife had to let two of the grooms go along with a lot of the other workers. The buggy barn is down to one man."

Eric gestured to Matthew to untie the horses from the hitching rack. He climbed laboriously into the front seat, took up the reins, and drove off with the golden dogs looking over his shoulder intently, scanning the landscape for other dogs to bark at.

Ryan Buchanan watched as they disappeared and rubbed his red chin thoughtfully. He kept the whiskers on his face long, to protect his pale Irish skin from the sun. "Most beautiful dogs I've ever seen. When did he get them?"

Matthew grinned. "He's been breeding those dogs and their predecessors for ten years."

"Were they always that beautiful?"

"Not only that, they're excellent hunting dogs as well. Would you like a pair?"

"Oh, yes. My wife is good with horses and dogs and would love them."

"I'll talk to Father. He has more dogs than he needs. His wife has been wanting to cut down on their expenses now."

Matthew looked at Ryan out of the corner of his eye, "What's this about children? You aren't too old. You're only 49."

"Yes, but women these days don't usually have children at that age."

"I didn't think she was that old."

Ryan shrugged. "No, but we've been trying to have children for several years without success."

Ryan had come to Annapolis in 1776 after Matthew had captured his ship and smuggled him into the country. Now he was a citizen and had run the shipyard for several years. He was married to Matthew's old school teacher, who came to the shipyard as a draftsman. She was now completely accepted by the men of the yard and drew all the plans for their ships. Elizabeth was well-featured, although not beautiful, and Ryan had found in her every answer to the end of his seagoing career.

Matthew said, "If you really want to adopt a child I'll try to help you. The mayor is an old schoolmate of mine and he runs the orphanage."

"The mayor? What does he have to do with it?" Ryan asked.

"As I said before, he's the head of the adoption agency. He runs it."

———

The next morning Eric's rig came flying up to the hitching rack, nearly carrying it away before he managed to get the two prancing horses under control. He climbed down slowly, rubbing his sore joints. "That damned buggy needs better springs! I'm sore," he said to Ryan.

"Where are your dogs?"

"Left them home for a session of obedience training. This will be a serious session, and they need it."

Matthew, John Paul, and Ryan joined him at a large table in the main office. Ryan spread out a set of plans.

"What's that?" Eric asked. He hated to try to read plans, preferring to build from rough sketches and oral orders.

Matthew said, "These are plans for our latest cargo ship now on the ways."

Eric smacked his hand on the sketches, "Beautifully drawn," he remarked, "but as a ship it won't do as a moneymaker in the new era."

"What do you mean?" asked Ryan.

"I spent all night thinking about the problems we will face in the coming decade."

"Can we hear about them?" Matthew asked.

"Well, for one thing," Eric explained, "I'm concerned that there will be a long period of quasi-war. The Congress will dither for years in spite of what was reported in yesterday's newspaper articles. I don't think these newly authorized ships will be at sea for quite a while."

"What then?" Matthew asked.

"We'll be up to our ears in privateers. We should be building the merchant ships the French and English will inevitably capture or sink as well as the privateers we will be needing soon."

Matthew questioned, "Then why don't you like our set of plans?"

"They're all right for the peacetime market, but we have to shift over to building ships for a war or a near war situation."

"Yes, and maybe capable of carrying a few guns," offered Ryan.

"This new market will soon see the light if we continue losing our merchant ships."

"It isn't too soon to build a new class of fast merchant ships capable of eluding the British and French warships."

"I agree, and the same hull will also be suitable for a new class of large privateer."

"What about getting in on building the new large frigates?" asked Matthew.

Eric laughed. "Much as I admire Joshua Humphreys, he can't help us directly. He'll have to allot construction to the large shipyards in the districts of the important congressmen."

Matthew said, "Just the same, I'd like to go up to see him."

"Of course, go ahead," agreed Eric, "he will have some good ideas about how to build a new large class of schooner hull to be used for both fast merchant ships and privateers. Take Martha. She needs to see the bright lights of Philadelphia. Take Ellen too."

Matthew laughed, "Whoa, my teenage daughters are tough. I'll have a time keeping her in line."

"True," said her grandfather, "but realize that something better might come along and make her less satisfied with the local lads. I've seen her riding; none of the locals will ever catch her on horseback."

"No, Father, but I worry about her. She's as beautiful as her mother but much more headstrong."

"Well, she comes of good stock. Just be careful that you watch her closely until you get her married off."

———

The next day as Eric, Ryan, and Matthew were going over the plans, Eric nudged Matthew. "Look at those two."
He pointed at Elizabeth and John Paul, leaning over a large drafting table. John Paul was busily drawing, and Elizabeth, leaning over him, was lending encouragement.

Matthew watched them for a few moments. Then he said, "She's obviously teaching him how to draw plans."

Ryan shrugged, "He already knows all there is to know about shipbuilding, and he has been to sea and seen action.

This will complete his qualifications for taking over the shipyard someday."

Matthew said, "He's been well qualifed for some time. This is something else. She looks like someone who is teaching her relief."

Ryan shrugged again, "Look closely at her."

Eric then noticed her beautiful complexion, her swelling bust, and her growing middle. "By God! That's it! She's pregnant!"

Ryan nodded. "That's right, but she didn't tell me until yesterday."

Eric said, "Then I take it she wants to turn over her drafting job draftsman to John Paul. But can he do it?"

Matthew said, "Easily. He has always drawn well."

"And I take it Elizabeth won't stay on as draftswoman any longer." Eric asked Ryan.

"No. This is her only chance to be a mother, and she wants to do it full time."

Matthew said, "I understand. I wish I'd been able to spend more time with my children."

Chapter 3

The captain of the packet took one last glowering look at the elder Christopher and his horses before ordering the mooring lines taken in and yelling at the boatswain to hoist sail. The fresh breeze moved the sleek little sloop out into the brown waters of the Severn River. When she was clear, the captain ordered a course set for the south. The passengers, mostly regulars, tried to find a quiet nook on deck in which to snooze. Others gathered in the small central cabin for the usual card games, which would last for the voyage's duration.

Matthew was standing as near to the wheel as he could without interfering with the movements of the captain, who noted his presence, recognizing a kindred seagoing spirit. He asked, "First trip, sonny?"

Matthew laughed. "No. I've made many. Some in my own ships."

The captain grinned, and cocked an eye aloft. "Then ye'll know enough to watch out for those harbor gulls up there. By the way, who was that crusty old gent who almost destroyed my brow with his wild horses?"

"That's my father. He's never mastered his horses, but he is good with a ship."

Matthew decided it was time to leave the captain alone and strolled towards Martha and Ellen who were leaning on the rail to watch the receding Annapolis skyline. As the packet gained way, the forest of church spires slowly disappeared behind the green western shore.

Ellen saw her father coming, curled her upper lip slightly, and demanded, "Papa, what do we do on this old bucket for the rest of the trip?" Ellen was changing from a smart young girl into a striking replica of her beautiful mother, though Ellen was a bit taller and a little thinner. Her dark brown hair was hanging down the back of her graceful neck, after the fashion of the young girls, but with her mother's help it was mostly swept up with a set of shining diamond clips, a gift from her father on her sixteenth birthday. The young men thought she was "smashing," like the British girls they had read about in the English novels or magazines occasionally available in Annapolis bookstores. Ellen was obviously far ahead of her contemporaries socially, but she tolerated them so well that they liked her.

Matthew smiled tolerantly. "Don't be so negative. This is a fast, sleek little ship, and our trip can be very pleasant if you'll let it be so."

"Yes, Father, but how long will it take?"

"Three hundred miles. We'll be making ten knots, and it will take thirty hours. We'll be in Philadelphia late tomorrow afternoon."

Martha looked anxiously at the passing water as it formed small waves that broke gently against the starboard side. "This is the first time I'll be going to sea."

Ellen signed, "Oh, Mother, this isn't really 'going to sea'. We're still in the Chesapeake Bay, and we will be here for a long time."

"That's so," Matthew said, "We'll be in the Chesapeake Bay all day and at dusk we will round Cape Charles and pass into the Atlantic Ocean. We'll continue up the coast all night and enter the Delaware Bay at about dawn. Near noon we'll pass the city of Wilmington and continue sailing up the Delaware River for a few hours to Philadelphia.

Ellen yawned. "Then I'll go to our stateroom, cram myself into that tiny upper berth, and catch up on my sleep." She went off to the only stateroom on the ship, which Matthew had managed to reserve with a small cash payment to the agent.

Matthew watched her go, thinking of her older sister. "Martha, I'm glad Mary is nicely settled in life."

Martha looked at him fondly. "I think she's an accomplished schoolteacher and a good wife."

Matthew snorted. "Will Ellen ever do as well?"

His wife sighed. "I hope so."

Matthew squinted, his eyes questioning. "Why is she sleepy at this time of the day?"

"Didn't you hear our piano being played late last night?"

"Hell, no. Why was it being played so late?"

"You don't pay enough attention to your children, or you'd know that Ellen must be home at nine." I've always told her that she can entertain her friends in our parlor any time."

"So they were singing with the piano?"

"Some, but mostly dancing. Ellen is a superb dancer, and you should dance with her sometime."

"My God! What next?"

"Nothing, I hope, or I'll have to send you down below to chaperone."

"Well, young people are a little different these days. Imagine doing that. We never did."

Martha giggled. "We certainly didn't. There weren't any dances in those days. You were working in the shipyard all day, and I was working as a waitress and an accountant in my family's restaurant."

Matthew smiled. "Those were tougher times when we were young, and then the war started."

Martha sighed. "I don't think you ever learned to dance, except for horn pipes and that sailor solo stuff."

"I can't do that 'sailor solo stuff' either. But I have at least learned to do a passable ballroom dance. I'll show you tomorrow."

"When did you learn to do that?"

"Before we were married. I assumed we'd have dancing at our wedding, and I didn't want to be unprepared."

"Well, aren't you the one! Who taught you?"

"You won't believe it. Elizabeth Cranston before she became Elizabeth Buchanan. She was good."

Martha was beginning to turn slightly pale as the waves increased in size and the ship responded to them. She gulped and said, "I'm going to join Ellen. Will you be all right with the other passengers?"

"Oh, yes. I've been with them before in the main cabin. There'll be a card game or two, but by the time we turn into the open sea and it gets rough they'll break up, and all the passengers will head for the bunks down below. I'll get into a good one early and skip the card games. I should get in several hours sleep since I'm used to the noise."

The first two legs of the trip passed peacefully, even with an easterly wind rolling the little ship markedly. At dawn, after the ship had turned into the quiet waters of the Delaware Bay, Matthew knocked on the stateroom door. A muffled voice answered, "Come in."

Matthew opened the door and passed in a covered tray. "Here are some biscuits, bacon, and apples."

Ellen groaned. "Take that greasy bacon away and leave the rest."

About noon the packet had reached the mouth of the Delaware River near the port of Wilmington, and the near violent motion of the ship had ceased. Matthew tried knocking again, and in a few minutes both Martha and Ellen appeared, stylishly dressed and ready for the shore.

Ellen said, "It's wonderful what a little sleep will do. Father, will you show me the sights along the river that you were bragging about?"

"Certainly," said Matthew.

Around noontime, after the group had been fortified with ham sandwiches and strong black coffee, Matthew led the ladies to the port rail forward. "That's the port of Wilmington," he said, pointing to a group of rusty tanks, piers, and decaying boat hulls along the river front.

Ellen sneered. "What's beautiful about that? Somebody should put a match to it."

Matthew continued, "As soon as we pass this portion of the river, we'll see the city's residential section. There are many nice estates on the waterfront and a park or two. Of course the business section and the larger residences are back from the river."

Ellen sniffed. "I should hope so. It smells terrible down here."

———

After gliding slowly up the river for two hours, Philadelphia came into view.

Martha asked, "How can we make such good time with so little wind?"

"Well," replied Matthew, "the wind is coming from astern and doesn't feel like much, but it is pushing us along at five knots. Last night we were making twelve at times and got a little ahead of schedule."

Mid-afternoon they saw the fast packet landing. The captain maneuvered his ship skillfully toward it, taking down his sails and turning broadside just in time to let the wind push his ship gently alongside the pier.

Martha observed, "That seemed too easy."

"He's done that landing hundreds of times. It isn't as easy as it looks," said Matthew.

He supervised the unloading of their baggage with the help of a young passenger, who was more than a little smitten with Ellen and had asked her to go dancing at the hotel that night.

 Martha cleared her throat loudly and said to the young man, "We'll be dining at the best hotel. You might drop by after dinner and we can talk about the dancing."

Ellen's suitor bowed to Martha and walked away. Once he was out of earshot, Ellen sighed, "Mother, you always interfere."

Martha shrugged. "I don't think I am all that bad. I always think that every night out with a young man in a strange city needs a little investigation. If he's as good as I think he is, he'll be back."

Matthew hired a carriage from a waiting line and asked the driver to take them to the best hotel in town. "Make sure it has a good restaurant," he added.

The driver grinned and said in his best Philadelphia accent, "Governor, we got lotsa good ones, and from the look of you I'm sure you like to eat."

Soon they pulled up at the entrance, and in half an hour they were established in the top suite of the hotel.

Matthew said, "Now you ladies have until seven o'clock to shop and dress for dinner. I'm going to catch up on my sleep. Then I'll take you down to dine."

"And tomorrow?" Martha asked.

"You will have all day to shop while I'm meeting with Joshua Humphreys. We take the packet home early the next morning." He looked intently at Ellen, "And if you aren't ready, young lady, I'm going to leave you here, and if I have to leave you it will be a long walk home."

Ellen shrugged. "I'll tell you tonight how I like it here, and I may have my gentleman caller bring me home if I like him that much and you insist on being ornery."

Dinner at the hotel dining room was elegant, served by expert white-gloved waiters. Ellen rolled her eyes as one waiter skillfully filled her water glass. "Nothing like this in Annapolis."

Martha frowned. "Mammy Sarah and her serving girls are just as good."

Ellen clarified, "I wouldn't say anything against Mammy Sarah. After all, she was with us before I was born."

Martha reflected, "The service at my parent's restaurant was good. Who needs white gloves?"

Matthew suggested that they order Maryland crab cakes and steaks. Martha looked slyly at Ellen when the crab cakes were served. "You see, Maryland has something that is good. These probably came from the waters off Annapolis."

Following an after-dinner stroll to see the windows of the big stores, the party returned to the hotel. Matthew yawned, "I've got to get to bed early."

Ellen looked pointedly at her mother and demanded, "Mother, you promised I could see the sights, and you practically arranged for me to go dancing with that young man from the packet. I noticed a sign in the lobby about dancing tonight. Are you going to let father get away with this?"

Martha laughed, "No, certainly not. Matthew you have to take us dancing."

Matthew looked at his watch resignedly. "All right. Until midnight."

Matthew did his best to dance with both ladies, but in half an hour the young passenger arrived and came to the table. He apologized for being late. He was properly dressed and appeared to be a match for Ellen. His slim six feet were topped with a shock of brown hair, suitably cut, and a handsome face with alert brown eyes and a straight nose. Martha guessed he would be a good dancer, and in fact he was an excellent one.

Soon he and Ellen were whirling around the floor in deep conversation.

Martha, watching them, said to her husband, "I think he'll do. He's a pleasant young man."

"My God! How can you make such a rapid judgement? He may be a swindler or even a thief."

Martha laughed. "Stop it! I can tell enough about him to feel safe in letting them get acquainted. The rest will follow. You must admit he is tall, well-dressed, and a good dancer." She giggled. "Better than you are."

"Better than how?"

"As a dancer."

"Oh, all right."

Matthew sighed with relief, "Now can I go up to bed?"

Martha laughed, "Oh, no. You promised to stay here until midnight, and I want to dance with you myself until then. Now let's go out to the floor."

"All right, but let's not twirl. I might fall over. We'll just do waltzes and fox trots."

"That's a good idea, I still have some 'sea legs' left."

At midnight Matthew stumbled up to bed, leaving Martha to chaperone what seemed to be a growing romance between Ellen and the young man. It turned out that he lived on a plantation near Annapolis, which made him increasingly acceptable. His name was Dresser Linthicum.

At seven o'clock the next morning after breakfast, Matthew left the ladies sleeping. He hired a carriage for the day and set off for the Humphreys' shipyard.

The same old man Matthew remembered was still at the entry gate and recognized Matthew. "Hello, laddy, how are you? You used to come here on a horse and now you're behind one. I knew you'd do well, and I see I'm right."

Matthew laughed. "May I see Mister Humphreys?"

"Of course. He'll always be in to you. Same old office. Hitch your horses out front."

Matthew walked into the familiar office and asked to see Joshua Humphreys.

A new and much younger secretary paused in her work and looked up at him. "Can I help you, sir?"

"I'm Matthew Christopher from Annapolis, and I'd like to call on Mister Humphreys."

The secretary rose and headed towards the door behind her, instructing Matthew to sit down. "I'll tell him you're here,"she said.

She disappeared into the inner office, and in a few minutes the familiar figure of Joshua Humphreys came trotting out. "My God, boy, I'm so glad to see you after all these years. Please come into my office."

Matthew sat down inside the elegantly appointed room he remembered from years ago. Humphreys ordered coffee, and both lit cigars. "Matthew, I don't know why you're here, but I hope you will stay all day. I want to show you the design of my new frigates and the work we've done so far on the one in my yard. The keel and futtocks are up, and from them we can see the outline of a newly designed hull."

"Oh, yes sir. I'd love that. Also, I would like to ask you some questions about shipbuilding in general."

"You came to the right place. I owe you a huge debt from

when you helped me in 1775 build the *Randolph*. As I remember it, you also helped meet the need for officers by volunteering to go to sea with Captain Biddle."

Matthew nodded, thinking about the days he had spent in the shipyard, swinging a heavy adze to build the ship. Then the many added weeks he had spent as lieutenant, out-fitting and manning the ship.

He noted that Humphreys' body and legs had thickened since he had last seen him, and his hair had receded slightly so that his heavy features appeared even more prominent.

Humphreys' strong face clouded as he stamped out his cigar and leaned over confidentially. "I have many pleasant memories of Captain Biddle. He was an excellent captain, and she was an equally excellent ship. I've spent many a sleepless night wondering what happened to her."

Matthew said soberly, "When her magazines blew up there must have been a design problem in the magazine, but there were no survivors, so we will never know."

Humphreys blew his nose loudly and wiped his eyes. "Well, let's go take a tour of the shipyard. We'll both feel better."

Chapter 4

Joshua led Matthew to the ways on which the frame of a very large ship was growing. They were the same ways on which Matthew had helped build a ship years ago, but they now had the capacity to hold a hull twice the size. Matthew shook his head in wonder and tried to imagine what the ship would look like when it was completely finished.

Humphreys stopped and pointed toward the ways. "There's my baby, the frigate *United States.*"

Matthew whistled. "She looks big enough to be a ship of the line."

"She'll be able to take on many of the smaller British ships of the line. Unless I miss my guess, or our Navy's intelligence is faulty, the British are going to keep on building the same type of frigate they have always built, and the French will follow right along. In the types of sea warfare I envision, we'll never see any British or French ships of the line close up. If our new frigates do, they'll simply outrun them."

Matthew nodded. "You mean the British ships of the line will never really leave the waters surrounding the islands of Great Britain?"

"More or less. They have gone as far as the Nile River in the Mediterranean, but they aren't suited for long voyages in the Pacific or the Atlantic. They have never had to be."

"I see," said Matthew.

"On the other hand, the speed and hull capacity of the new ships will allow them to range and rule the seas of the world."

"But won't you need many?"

"I figure about six. That's all we will ever get the Congress to fund anyway. Once the French and the British find out what they can do, they'll avoid them."

"I see your point." Matthew said, idly rubbing the

smooth finished surface of a nearby scantling. "Please tell me more about them. All the timbers I can see appear to be much larger than the ones I worked on."

Joshua laughed. "Almost double in proportion, but size alone isn't the secret of strength. Although I must say, our frigates will be about one and a half times the outer dimensions of the British or French frigates."

Matthew whistled. "Look at the futtocks, called ribs by Americans. These mighty ribs are the size of the ones I worked on, and the scarf joints you used here seem as strong as the pieces they join."

"Much stronger. You can't find natural wood bent-pieces in the forests any more. They all have to be built from smaller pieces."

"And why are these scantlings between the futtocks? Are they holding them in place temporarily?"

Humphreys shook his head. "No. They are far more than braces. They will be permanent pieces of the framing, diagonal braces between the futtocks. Something new in design. And they will enable the planking, after it is put into place, to double the hull's ability to withstand cannon balls."

Matthew whistled. "Almost like iron. What will her dimensions be?"

"At about 1500 tons, a length of 175 feet and a beam of 43 feet, I estimate she will still do eleven knots, and maybe more in a good wind."

"That means no ship can catch her."

"No."

Matthew laughed. "The *Mary* certainly could, and any other schooner rigged ship, but they'd have no business getting near her."

"What is her armament?"

"Thirty-two 24-pounders. They will also be able to carry twenty-four 42-pound carronades. Big, blunt guns with limited range, but real killers in close."

"That doesn't seem like many guns."

"Don't be fooled. These ships will be capable of employ-

ing and supporting as many as 56 guns. I don't think it will
be long before the Congress appropriates money for more
guns when the captains ask for it."

"Will they get it?"

"Certainly." Matthew shook his head. "I wouldn't care to
fight The *Mary* except with another of your ships. Captain
John Paul Jones would love the speed of this one."

Humphreys led Matthew back a few yards from the looming skeleton, so they could get a better overall view. "Look
at her outline. She will be longer and beamier than the
British frigates and still be much faster. Look at the height
of her hull. The bulwarks will be at least three feet lower
than those of our present frigates and even the French and
British frigates. She's long, low, and mean."

Matthew shrugged. "Yes, sir, I agree with you. She'll
sweep the seas. I don't believe a single ship can stand up to
her. I would like to learn more from you about building
ships. I'm afraid I am out of date."

"Come with me," said Humphreys.

In a few moments they were comfortably seated again
with fresh coffee and cigars.

Humphreys smiled. "Fire away. Maybe I can help."

"Well, our shipyard has struggled through the recent lean
years, losing money steadily, and it now needs to take a new
direction, or we will be facing bankruptcy. Like you, my
father foresees a market for bigger and faster merchant ships
which are ready for conversion to privateers, should the
opportunity or need arise."

Humphreys nodded his large head vigorously. "Your
father is quite right. Design and build bigger and faster merchant ships even if the prospective buyers don't have enough
foresight to want them. I agree we'll be in a quasi-war or a
full war within a year or two. You may use any of my innovations. Build all of your merchant ships for easy conversion,
and take the small loss of cargo capability. For your purpose,
stick to schooner rigs. If you are building any square-rigged
ships, get rid of them as soon as you can. They will be slow

and cumbersome."

"You seem to agree completely with my father," said Matthew.

"Yes, he's a wise old man. You take after him. I suppose you appreciate that in spite of what you may have read in the papers, I can't assign the building of any large naval ships to you. They will be completely controlled by the Congress in spite of my high-sounding title. The Congress is both a roadblock and a demanding overseer. It is slowed severely by the members who demand more control in the name of constitutional authority, though they usually act for personal reasons."

"I won't repeat this."

"I'll say it out loud."

"You mean you'll say they do it for money?"

"Yes. For money. I'd like to horsewhip many of them and even shoot some of them."

Matthew noticed that Humphreys had grown heated and was shaking slightly, so he decided to change the subject.

"Would my shipyard get any of the smaller ships from the Congress?"

"If more smaller ships are ever authorized, you will be the first to be considered. Now let's go up the pike for some beer and lunch. I want to hear all about your adventures during the old days at sea with John Paul Jones."

As they walked up the pike, Matthew said, "I have one last favor to ask of you."

"Anything."

"I have a second son, Bruce. He wants very much to go to sea in a naval ship."

"And why not on your own merchant ships? That's where the money will be."

"That's not what he wants. Not enough action. He's been at sea every summer. He's well-qualified in seamanship and navigation. Good physique. He'll make a fine midshipman on the *United States*."

Humphreys counted on his fingers. He'll be the right

age. She'll be taking on a crew in the spring of '98. I make him 16 then."

"Right. He'll be in Saint John's College until then."

"Don't worry. I'll speak to Captain Barry about him. He'll jump at the chance to get such a fine young man. They're hard to find."

Lunch was a pleasant interlude in an interesting day, and Matthew knew that with his questions answered he shouldn't take any more of Humphreys' time.

After a cordial departure, he returned to the hotel to find that Ellen had been out all day with her new beau. Matthew looked at her with a calculating eye. "I take it that you are mine for the rest of the afternoon?"

"No, Father, I'm bound for a tea dance."

Matthew grinned. "I see I'm in the rear rank now."

Ellen laughed. "Maybe even farther back. I'll keep you informed of your position."

"I'll count on it."

After Ellen departed in a flurry of pleated skirts, petticoats, and powder, Matthew looked at Martha, "I suppose you'd like to go for a walk?"

Martha laughed. "Some sailor on leave you are. Lock the door and come over here."

Later that afternoon, as she lay in his arms, he told her of his conversation with Humphreys regarding Bruce. She moved away from him. "Damn! All you men are alike."

"What do you mean?"

"All you do is cause trouble. Here I thought my two youngest would stay safely at home with me."

Matthew sighed patiently. "So did I, but all men are made differently. You will still have Rob Roy, the youngest."

"But Bruce is just a boy."

"He'll be a man soon, and he will want to see the world and even fight a little."

"But you know how dangerous that will be for him, and

you say he will be a midshipman."

"Yes."

"And just what does 'midshipman' mean?"

"A midshipman is a very junior officer, stationed during battles in the middle or center part of the ship, passing orders from the quarterdeck aft to the officers forward. Some midshipmen have other battle stations."

"And the ones in the middle are out in the open and good targets for fire of every kind?"

"Only when the action is close enough."

"And we can't keep him from going to sea?" Martha implored.

"I don't think we should stand in his way."

"He could still be killed by shots passing over the deck."

"Certainly, but the others are in the same danger."

Martha began to cry softly. "I don't like any of it. Why can't he just build ships and let the others go to sea" She implored?

"Bruce will be on a ship that will never sink."

"I've heard that before."

"All right. We have a couple years left to enjoy him. Maybe we'll have more children."

Martha laughed despite her tears. "Not a chance."

"Why not?"

"Mammy Sarah has given me a new potion to prevent such a thing from happening."

Matthew stared at her in astonishment.

"Are you using it?" he asked curiously.

Martha blinked her eyes. "Haven't you noticed that we haven't had any children since Rob Roy?"

Matthew sighed. "And here I thought I was just getting older. Good night, dear."

Soon Matthew was sleeping, as Martha cried quietly into her pillow. It was not the first time she had cried over a man, but this was different. Matthew was a strong, capable man, but Bruce and Rob Roy were still her babies, and she was crying over them.

Chapter 5

The voyage back to Annapolis was pleasant. Ellen's young friend was along, so she was a lot more lively than on the way north.

Matthew noticed and managed to steal a few minutes of her attention. "Ellen, can you tell me a little about your beau?"

"Father, I don't know much about him except what he told me. He is from an Annapolis family, and he hopes to have me meet them soon. All you need to know now is that I like him. He is intelligent, handsome, charming, a good dancer, a lover of horses, and he is not overly forward."

"I hope you like him for all those qualities in that order."

Ellen shrugged. "That's about right, but don't hold me to it. Can we talk about this some other time? I want to get back to him."

After they arrived, Matthew went directly to the shipyard office to talk to his father.

Martha reminded him, "We dine at seven. We'll have grits and steak. Our guests include our Congressman."

The horses were tied in front, busily emptying nosebags of oats provided by Elizabeth Buchanan.

Matthew went into the office, and Eric greeted him. "How was the trip? Anybody seasick?"

Matthew laughed. "No, but I think Ellen has become just a little lovesick."

"Who's the culprit?"

"A young man named Dresser Linthicum. She's been with him steadily for the last two days. Do you know anything about him?"

Eric's eyebrows shot up. "Good family. Lots of money. Big estate filled with fine horses, more than my wife has, and some actually win races. Come to think of it, the boy used to be a jockey. Won a lot of races. I think he is a very handsome young man with pleasant mannners."

"He has grown a lot physically since he was a jockey. Ellen seems to be completely smitten."

"You are lucky."

"That should relieve my concern on the home front. Now for business."

Eric sat up. "Good or bad?"

"Neither. My visit with Joshua Humphreys was very pleasant but not completely productive."

"And?"

"As we suspected, we probably won't be assigned to build any very large naval vessels, at least not anytime soon."

"For the reasons we suspected?"

"Of course."

"Damn! We've got to get into the pockets of the Maryland congressmen."

"Won't work. Baltimore will be a big port some day. But the Maryland shipyards can't compete with Philadelphia, Portsmouth, Boston, and New York. I'll tell you Joshua's opinion of congressmen later."

"The damned northern bankers control everything."

"Sure, it all starts with money, and in the North banks are on every corner. Joshua held forth in a diatribe about the Congress. I may as well tell you now."

"Anybody in particular?"

"He thinks the large majority of them are scoundrels. He didn't pick out any one in particular. He certainly didn't mention our local congressman, who is coming to dinner tonight."

"Good. That may mean he's on our side."

"With his hands in our pockets?"

Eric shrugged. "That's standard for business and politics."

Well, son, we still have lots of shots to fire. We build and sail ships better than others do. We have to figure out a way to make money using our talents and not fall behind the competition. What did Joshua Humphreys say about that?"

"He didn't mention competition."

"Why not?"

"He doesn't consider that a problem. If we do what you and he expect us to do, you'll leave the competiton behind, so it won't be a problem."

"Anything else?"

"He agreed with your ideas about the future, saying that our future, like his, is in shipbuilding."

"What did he mean by that?"

"He was talking about one of the six new frigates, the *United States*."

"She will run over any French or British frigate on the seas, or run away from a squadron of them if she chooses."

"Will the six be enough to re-establish America's control of the seas?"

"I think so. If you see one of them, you'll think the same."

"But how will this help us?"

"That particular ship won't, but it's design is the general answer."

"I don't follow you."

From now on we need to build long, low, fast schooners that are much larger than the last one. I know they won't be square-rigged like the big new frigates, and they won't be the most efficient cargo carriers. But I want to build a schooner no frigate of any size can catch. Put a half dozen stern-chasers on her, and I'll take her anywhere full of cargo and bring her back the same way."

"I take it you realize we'll stand to make less profit per voyage."

"Yes, of course, but the profit will be certain and the voyages will be shorter."

"I see. One or the other."

"No, both."

Eric sat pondering for a few minutes. Then he leaped out of his chair so fast he seemed to have forgotten his rheumatism. "We can do it! We'll finish this ship as soon as we can and sell it. Tomorrow you, John Paul, Ryan, and Elizabeth must gather here and start the plans for the next ship to be built just like you want it."

"Why tomorrow? Why not now?"

"Because I think your wife deserves one day with you as does mine with me. When we start this, I wouldn't expect to leave the office day or night until we're finished. Our wives won't see much of us."

"All right. There's one more thing. I want you to hear this from me before Bruce or Martha tells you. I've made arrangements with Joshua to have Bruce appointed as a midshipman on the *United States*."

Eric grinned. "Bruce will be exultant, but Martha will kill you."

"She knows, and she didn't."

"Well I'd keep my back away from her for a while. She might stick a knife in it."

———————

The next days were feverish. Occasionally Ryan took a look outside to make sure the work on the ship was progressing. Then he rejoined the others as they all bent over the large table, rapidly filling with papers that were covered with curves and lines. To the unskilled, they meant little, but to the small group they became a beautiful entity, a large, graceful hull. One of the papers carried the plans for her rigging. Separate sheets were allotted for each deck of the ship, showing the placement of all guns and rigging. Another paper showed a side view, and still others presented the ship from the bow with sectional drawings along the length of the keel. Some were filled with duller material, dimensions, weights, material lists.

Gradually the lines became a ship. "Looks like the *Mary*," Eric observed.

"Yes, but a lot bigger," Elizabeth said.

Matthew nodded. "Yes, at least half again as big as she was. Just like the *United States*, she'll be strong and fast. The schooner rig will let me fight her, if necessary, with half the men the square-rigger on the ways will need."

———•·•———

Within two months the old ship slid down into the water of the Severn, and after two months of fitting out, she was sold to a group of Annapolis merchants.

Matthew watched her go. "Good riddance."

Eric said rationally, "They paid for her in full, and we needed the money for materials."

John Paul finished his calculations based on the volumes of records he had kept. "Ten percent profit," he announced, "and that's not enough."

Matthew shook his head, "You're right. Not enough. We need to make at least forty percent, and we will make even more in the future."

Eric nodded. "I agree. Now let's lay the keel for the new *Mary*."

"Same name?" asked Matthew.

"Of course. After my mother and the last ship I commanded."

The keel grew rapidly and then the futtocks sprouted like giant mushrooms. Matthew demonstrated the Joshua method of splicing the pieces of the futtocks. Eric stared with admiration. "I'll be damned. Why didn't I think of that?"

Matthew explained, "You didn't need to splice them in the old days because naturally bent wood was readily available in the forests. Now it has all been used."

———•·•———

Another similar hull was started in their Chestertown shipyard across the bay, run by older brother Kevin. Chestertown was slightly smaller than Annapolis, but there were many watermen and builders living along the eastern shore waterfront and the surrounding area. Many took jobs with the shipbuilding company just as their fathers and grandfathers before them. Kevin had no trouble finding plenty of men to build good ships.

"We'll still use the same plans," Eric announced to

Matthew. "I'll put Scotty MacIntosh in command of her. She'll be named the *Martha* after your wife."

Gradually the construction of the *Mary* pulled ahead. "Looks like the spring of 97," Eric determined. "Let's plan for a single launching celebration for both ships. You can begin to recruit your crew now."

Matthew laughed. "I have to fight them off. All the seamen within a hundred miles who have seen the hull of this ship want to join her crew."

Eric pursed his lips. "You'll have a lot of good candidates. Pick good men."

"I will. I'll have no trouble."

Chapter 6

The framework was completed in the late fall with the decking and side planking put in place. All of the nearby saw pits and steam powered mills were operating at capacity. The newer circular saws ran on English steam engines powered by overhead belts and transmission axles, with much of the steam fueled by the mounds of adze shavings that had been collected for years.

Annapolis had been the leading shipbuilding center of the Chesapeake Bay area during the Revolutionary War, when two-thousand privateers from frigates to rowing galleys had been produced. After the war, Annapolis remained the leading building center for large ships, the Christopher Shipyard built the most. Many chandlers remained in the Annapolis area after the war and catered to merchant ships using the port. Rope walks and sail lofts could be found in the area north of town and remained there for years. Most foundry work was shifted to foundries in Baltimore and Philadelphia and guns were imported from England. Eric, foreseeing periods of international tension when he would not be able to acquire guns from England, made a deal with a leading foundry in Pittsburgh. He offered to obtain small amounts of good quality iron ore, copper, and coke, and he even brought over a leading gun designer. The Dutchman claimed to be able to produce a gun, using the superb ingredients he was promised, that would increase the range of a comparable gun by three or four hundred yards. Eric salivated over the possibility of success and what his ships could do with these guns.

As Eric paced up and down, looking at the emerging new hull, Matthew noted his impatience. "What's the matter, Father?"

"The masts. You said you'd get them, but they aren't here. I don't see anything up there but blue sky."

Matthew laughed. "Calm down. They'll be here soon. When I went to see Joshua Humphreys we made a deal about the masts. There's a ship coming from the Adriatic with a load of live oak logs that can be shaped into first class masts. It will unload six at our shipyard at Chestertown, six here, and the rest at Humphreys' yard in Philadelphia. Obviously he will take the larger ones because his bigger ships will need them."

"And you'll get enough for six ships?"

"Yes, three ships at each yard with two masts each. A three year supply."

"Thank God. Now I can worry about something else."

"Try ironware. We're a little behind. Go over to Grisham Ironmonger Company and bang on the counter."

Eric whistled for his dogs. They hurtled out of the office door in a golden blur, eager for a ride. "If Grisham doesn't produce, I'll sic them on him."

———

As Matthew predicted, the live oak masts arrived in a week and were soon shaped and put in place where they were held securely by shrouds and ratlines.

The sails had already been cut and sewn by a leading sail maker and stored in a nearby warehouse. The halliards and sheets used to control the sails were made with rope from an Annapolis rope walk. All were added to the growing pile of canvas and rigging.

When Eric felt that the masts and wooden parts were varnished and properly dried, he ordered the sails and rigging brought aboard and put in place. He ordered the sails run up on a calm day and looked carefully at the cut and drape of the hanging canvas. "It'll do," he said. "They're cut and sewn well, but only wind in them will truly tell the tale."

The sails were taken down and stowed below. Matthew's boatswain, a man he had sailed with before, smiled as he strolled about the decks on other business. Matthew grinned at Bostwick. "You look like a pregnant woman."

"Aye, and I feel like one." Bostwick said. "A boatswain

with good sails below always wants to see them given birth and tested. I think they'll do."

Bostwick was an older man with much experience at sea, but Matthew knew he needed to add youth to his officer group because soon he would have to promote one of them to command .

Much work still had to be done. The stern chasers were brought from Philadelphia by barge and were then hoisted aboard and rigged. Also, balls and powder were put in the carefully constructed magazines.

Eric had tried hard to have the new foundry in Pittsburgh provide the guns for the *Mary*, but the head of the foundry had complained that he needed several more months to test the guns.

Eric asked, "Why so long?"

"Because I want the guns to be the best possible product. If I gave them to you too early and they blew up, you'd want your money back."

Eric laughed. "I don't think so. Make them both long range and safe. I'll wait."

Matthew remembered the *Randolph* and her devastation just after he had left the ship. He chose a veteran gunner from the Annapolis retired community and persuaded him to go to sea one last time. Velasquez had served in the Spanish Navy and was known as a skilled and safe gunner. He was swarthy and heavy-bearded. His face was marred by a long scar down his right cheek, which drew down his eye slightly but did not hinder his vision. The total effect was ominous when he was seen for the first time, but Matthew had found him to be a rare combination of skill and tenacity, an individual full of compassion for the young sailors he trained.

There were many items listed in the group's meticulous original plans that were now being taken from the warehouses and brought aboard. Anchors, their large hempen cables, extra cordage for emergency repairs, a cooking area, and many seemingly unimportant but necessary items were carefully inventoried by John Paul as they were put in their assigned places. After all the pieces of iron had been placed, a binnacle and compass werebrought aboard and it was then compensated as best as Matthew and the boatswain could.

"The ship will have to be swung at sea for a final compass compensation before we can use it," the boatswain said,

Matthew nodded. "The first thing we'll do as we go to sea."

At the height of the activity in the shipyard, Ellen rebelled and Matthew had to turn his attention to his daughter.

"What's wrong with Ellen?" he asked Martha early one morning.

"She won't get up," Martha sighed, shaking her head.

Matthew bristled. "I'll get her up just like I used to with a sound whack on her backside."

"Oh, no you won't. She's no longer a young girl. She's grown up now. She wants to withdraw from school and marry Dresser Linthicum."

"And she's rebelling by staying in bed?" roared Matthew.

"Yes. She has your attention now, and you can look in on her if you want to, but be gentle. That should guarantee better results than your usual sailor's swearing. She's heard that all her life."

"Can't Mammy Sarah do anything with her? After all, she raised her from a baby."

Martha stiffened. "Raising her is not the same as taking care of her. I've done that, and so have you when you've had the time. Besides, I think Mammy Sarah is on Ellen's side. They sometimes stay in her room and giggle for hours. Then they come down to the kitchen, make tea, and giggle some more."

"All right. Apparently some of the women of the house are against me. I'll look in on her."

Matthew went upstairs to Ellen's bedroom. By the time

he had climbed three flights of stairs, he had calmed down and had little breath left with which to launch his usual swearing session.

He knocked politely on Ellen's door.

"Yes, Father, I know you're there. Come in. But swearing at me will do no good."

Matthew pushed open the door and walked over to Ellen's bed. He sat down, bent over, and kissed her affectionately. "Now, tell me your troubles."

Ellen was astonished, and her green eyes flashed, reminding Matthew of his mother's eyes. They had been passed down to both women by some ancient Gaelic ancestor. "My God, Father," Ellen said, "are you really planning to listen to me?"

"Yes, Dear. Your Mother reminded me that you are now grown up and want to make your own decisions."

"Yes, and that's why I'm still in bed. I had to get your attention."

"You got it. Now tell me your plans."

"If you'll get up, I'll go over behind the screen and dress while we talk. I really want to get outside on this lovely day. I have a lot to do."

"Such as?"

"I have to withdraw from school first. Then I have to see Mrs. Linthicum and tell her I plan to accept Dresser's proposal."

"For what?"

"Marriage, of course, and don't say I'm too young. My Mother married you when she was 18."

"I guess you're right. I have only one request. Have your wedding after my ship is launched and before we leave on our first cruise."

Ellen giggled from behind the screen as her night dress flew over the top and onto the floor. There was the sound of splashing water. "I've been planning it that way. I want you to be around to give me away."

———•———

When Matthew got to the shipyard office, Eric was waiting with the latest Philadelphia paper, ready to explain its
contents to his son. "Here it is, December of 1796. The
world is changing. In June, a six-month truce was established between the U.S. and Tunis, and in November a
treaty of peace was concluded with the Bashaw of Tripoli.
Because of all this, the Congress has decided to suspend the
building of three of the new frigates."

Matthew said, "Still, President Washington wasn't fooled
and urged the Congress to increase naval strength."

"Yes, and on the 25th a French privateer fired on the
merchant ship the *Commerce.*"

Matthew sighed. "It's just a matter of time. Now let's get
to work. I have to get the ship finished before I launch my
daughter."

"What? Is that an announcement?" asked Eric.

"Yes. Young Linthicum."

"Ah," said Eric.

"Yes, he's the culprit," Matthew added.

"He's no culprit. He's a magnificent catch."

"I know, that was just an expression."

"Now we'll all have to work faster."

Chapter 7

In 1796, as a war storm gathered in Europe and the Caribbean, Matthew thought about his past fighting experience. He remembered vividly his months and years of fighting the British, both in a privateer and as a lieutenant in the Continental Navy. First, he had served in the *Randolph* and then in the *Ranger*, building her under Captain John Paul Jones, and then shifting to the outfitting of the *Bon Homme Richard*. Then he had returned to captain his own privateer, *Mary*, to capture the very British frigate that had driven his father's ship ashore in the Delaware Bay. He shook his head and tried to return to the present. He knew he had plenty of problems to solve without pondering past events.

At breakfast, Matthew ate hurriedly, anxious to leave for work. Sitting across from him, Martha cleared her throat. It was a mannerism that Matthew knew well, and he sighed patiently. He sat back and asked for another cup of coffee. He knew he was about to hear something that might upset his whole day, yet he deeply loved his wife and his family, and he knew he had to listen no matter what it was. "Yes, Dear," he said patiently. "Go ahead. I'm listening."

Martha carefully wiped her pretty lips. "Matthew, you need to concentrate more on Ellen's wedding.

"What! I thought we had plenty of time."

"Two weeks."

"My God! That's right around the corner!"

"It is. I know how preoccupied you've been, but your daughter is more important than your ship."

Matthew sat foward, nearly spilling his coffee. "All right. You have my full attention. Now tell me what I need to know."

"The date is fifteen days off."

"And I trust it will be a beautiful spring day. They all are in this month."

Martha nodded. "I hope so. As the mother of the bride, it is my responsibility to make all the arrangements, and as you know, I've been working hard."

Matthew grinned. "I'll be praying for the weather. Go ahead."

"Fortunately Ellen has been very cooperative and hasn't demanded much. I've gotten along well with the groom's family. Mrs. Linthicum is very nice, and we're fortunate to be getting such a wonderful son-in-law."

"The wedding dress?"

"Beautiful and almost ready. Mammy Sarah has helped a lot. You know what a good seamstress she is."

"Oh, yes. I remember your beautiful gown. Where will the wedding be?"

"Saint Anne's Church. The Vicar is ready. The reception will be held in our home and garden, and Jones Jebediah has agreed to bring most of his restaurant staff for the occasion."

Matthew chuckled. "I'll be glad to see my old shipmate. I understand his restaurant is doing well. And what will his father, old Jebediah, be doing?"

"He will drive Ellen to the church, just as he drove me to our wedding."

"Very well. Where is the couple going on their honeymoon?"

"The honeymoon is the business of the groom, and don't ask him any embarrassing questions about it."

Matthew sighed. "I hope the marriage ceremony will be fancier than ours was."

Martha nodded. "Ours was quick and simple, all right, but it was still wonderful."

"We didn't have much choice. I had to get to the shipyard in Philadelphia as soon as possible. My father was very anxious. At least we got through it and then left quickly on our honeymoon."

"Oh, yes I loved it."

Matthew sighed. "The trip in a wagon and horses up to

Philadelphia was a little trying on you."

Martha giggled. "The happiest days of my life. I enjoyed every minute of them. And now that you are in such a good mood, go to work."

The next two weeks were very busy for Matthew. He left most of the arrangements for the ship's completion in the hands of his father and Ryan Buchanan. He concentrated on the preliminaries of Ellen's wedding. Many of the leading families of Annapolis insisted on entertaining, and he found himself becoming more and more attracted to his future son-in-law and his family.

The beautiful Annapolis spring days marched on. Matthew spent some nights after social affairs at the shipyard, but the majority of his days and evenings were spent with his family. When the wedding day arrived, he was exhausted and happy.

Ellen was beautiful in her wedding gown, and the anxious groom was handsome in a suit of black velvet. Saint Anne's Church was amply decorated with flowers. The mayor had cooperated with Eric Christopher, and he ordered all carriages off the circle surrounding the church except for those of the wedding party and attendees. The entire town seemed to clear the decks for the important afternoon.

The ceremony was performed flawlessly. Later the proud father of the bride declared the affair to have been "taut and seamanlike."

Martha raised her black eyebrows. "I don't know what that naval expression means, but it was beautiful and made me very happy."

The reception was attended by all the leading citizens of Annapolis. Jones Jebediah's staff scurried about with refreshments, and Jebediah passed among the guests to make sure the service was adequate. Annapolis oysters and crabs were served in a dozen varieties of dishes, and delicacies flowed endlessly as Jebediah's chef took over the kitchen.

Midway in the affair, Dresser approached Matthew with a joyful yet determined look in his eye, "Sir, may I have a few words with you in private?"

Matthew looked at him questioningly. "What's the matter, son. Is the honeymoon off?"

Dresser laughed. "No, sir. And I won't be neglecting the bride as soon as our business is settled."

Matthew looked at Ellen, surrounded by young men. "Neglect her, and you'll be lucky to steal her away in time for the honeymoon. Now, what's the trouble?"

"I want to talk to you about cargo. I doubt you've had time to think much about the subject, but I've spent a lot of time considering it. My college courses at King William School were in business and commerce, and I've also done a lot of outside research. After the honeymoon, I hope to establish an export-import business with headquarters in Annapolis and with offices in Baltimore, Philadelphia, and Chestertown. I'll be in business to serve you and many others. I also hope to establish offices in the Caribbean area."

"Don't you need money for all that?"

"Yes, but not from you. I'd like for you to invest in my business at some future date so you can make more money. I understand your business is in very serious trouble. And, right now I have sufficient capital to start my business and begin operations."

"In spite of what you think, I can give you all the financial support you may need, and of course you will have my business. I am pleasantly surprised to hear all this, and I must confess that I am behind in making arrangements for export and import for my first voyages."

"I take it you will accept me as the head of the new business, and you will be my first customer?"

"Certainly. Your first assignment will be the cargo of the *Mary*."

"I agree, sir. And I'd like to go along with you on your first voyage. I'll set up my office in Havana, where I assume you will visit first. I'd like to serve as seaman on your ship during the voyage."

Matthew chuckled. "I admire your spirit, but you can't do that. You will be considered a junior officer, and I'll try to teach you all I can about seamanship and cargo stowage on the trip. There will be lots of time."

Dresser nodded eagerly. "I can navigate and sail small vessels well."

Matthew looked over at his daughter, now dancing with a succession of young men. "But how will your bride feel about your absence on a cruise? She's pretty headstrong."

"She is, but we've already reached an agreement. She's going back to school to complete her studies while I'm away."

Matthew whistled. "Great balls of fire in the rigging! You've done that! I tried to get her to finish school for over a year without success. Won't you pay a price?"

"Sure. We've made arrangements. Ellen wants to get involved in the business end of horsebreeding. My father has agreed to take her on after she graduates, and she will still have time to devote to my business."

Matthew shook his head. "Amazing!"

"Not necessarily so. I made a sort of trade with my father. He always wanted me to take over his business. I like horses, but that wasn't all I wanted. He has already begun to think of Ellen as the daughter he never had and they get along together fine."

"If this had happened on my forecastle I doubt if I would even have noticed it."

Dresser laughed. "You have been very busy, and we didn't want to bother you. Your wife knows all about it. Ask her tonight. Now I've got to get back to my beautiful bride."

Chapter 8

While Ellen and Dresser were on their short honeymoon, Eric, Matthew, and their shipyard crew labored to complete the *Mary*. On the 4th of July, to the accompaniment of fireworks and appropriate selections played by the town band, the *Mary* was launched before a large crowd of friends.

Almost before the crowd dissipated, workmen swarmed aboard and began the completion of the rigging. As other men brought miscellaneous equipment aboard, John Paul set up shop at the top of the brow to account for the the numbers and costs of all items brought aboard.

In the shipyard office, Matthew began to interview men who wanted to join the *Mary's* crew. Many asked, "When will you make her into a privateer?"

Matthew asked one, "Is that the only reason you want to join the crew of the *Mary?*"

Most freely admitted they were after the money, and he had to make hard choices over some of them. He valued their honesty. "I'd think they were darn fools if they didn't want to get ahead," he said to Eric. "But that must not be the chief reason."

"Do your best, son. They are all fine young men, and you can't go far wrong with any of them."

Many were sons of men who had sailed with Matthew, and some of the older men appeared and asked to be signed on as petty officers. All had shared in, or had heard of, the prize money the original *Mary* had won under Matthew's command during the Revolutionary War.

Matthew's standard reply, was, "I'm hoping to someday if the international situation continues to deteriorate, but for the first voyage, she will be a merchantman."

Nevertheless, many good men signed on, hopeful that they would be there when the situation changed.

Matthew then completed the appointment of his officers.

He selected two young men to be his lieutenants, whom he had known for several years, and they had been to sea as seamen. They were Lars Jensen and Angus MacClaren. Jensen was a husky, blond man of Norwegian descent. His flaxen hair turned almost white at sea and his normally light skin turned a dark bronze. When he came ashore the girls gathered around him like bees around honey. He spoke Norwegian and came from a family running a farm north of Annapolis. A boyhood of cleaning up after cows convinced him that the sea was not only cleaner but smelled better.

MacClaren was a Scotsman whose family had recently come to this country and found a better life. Angus thought he could make more money by going to sea and winning prizes if they ever became legal. In the meantime, he was waiting patiently and learning to become a better officer. Matthew thought he was lucky to have him but also thought he would develop more slowly than Jensen.

Velasquez the ship's gunner knew all about firing guns and, just as importantly believed in the safety of magazines and their contents. He was a middle-aged ex-Spanish navy gunner. After some effort had he been coaxed to come out of retirement. He was husky but of short-legged build.

Barry Bostwick, who had served with Matthew several years at sea and who had also been in charge of the rigging loft in the shipyard, was glad to get to sea again. Barry Bostwick's wife was badgering him, and he needed a change of scene. The years in the shipyard had left him with a slight potbelly, and he was determined to get rid of it.

The last officer, whom Matthew considered the most important to the future of his ship, was Jeremy Jarrell. Jarrell had been at sea for a few years as a seaman and had come ashore to start his education at King William School. Unfortunately his father had died, leaving Jarrell to support his mother. He had been forced to leave school and had asked Matthew for a job. "I need the money," he had said, "or I would have completed my education." Matthew hired him on the spot, feeling lucky to get the handsome, intelligent six foot tall man.

He was two hundred pounds of solid muscle, an indication of Jarrell's physical stamina that might be useful during long periods of storm and battle.

Matthew sent him home to consult with his mother and to say goodbye to her if he decided to accept the appointment. Jarrell returned the next morning with his sea gear and told Matthew that he accepted the appointment. Matthew gave him six months worth of wages to send over to his mother and felt he had gotten a gold mine in the young officer.

One morning Eric came racing into town behind his prize horses and skidded into his usual stop in front of the office hitching rack. He stomped into the office while Elizabeth scurried outside to take care of his horses. Eric asked, "Matthew, what's this I hear about the damned French again?"

Matthew gestured toward the latest Philadelphia paper lying on the drafting table. "Read it, and please don't curse too loudly. Elizabeth will be back in a moment, and she doesn't like strong language."

Eric shrugged his shoulders and then read from the newspaper. "'An American schooner seized by a French privateer.' Won't our politicians do anything? Here it is February and you are almost ready to go to sea."

"I'll go in April regardless."

The shipyard personnel worked overtime, and even some crew members were recruited to ready and load the ship.

In March another newspaper issue revealed that the "French had decided that Americans serving in enemy ships would be considered pirates, and U.S. ships not having crews listed in proper order would be considered lawful prizes."

Eric strode up and down the drafting room. "What the hell does that mean?"

Elizabeth tried to calm him wih a fresh cup of coffee, but he ignored it. The paper also announced that two more American ships had been seized. When Eric read the article, Elizabeth diplomatically left to take care of his horses, leaving him to his sulphurous cursing.

By the first of April 1797, Matthew got the *Mary* underway and sailed around in the bay training his crew in sailing the ship. When he was far enough out in the bay not to disturb nearby residents, he worked the men detailed to the stern chase guns, teaching them to load and aim the guns, then firing them at barrel targets.

Dresser now had a full manifest of cargo, provided by merchants as far away as Baltimore and Philadelpia, and many wagons began to arrive at the fitting out dock.

Matthew declared the ship ready to go to sea, and the cargo on the piers was loaded as rapidly as it arrived. Dresser and John Paul kept careful track of it, and Eric insisted on supervising the stowage below. "Can't be too careful," he announced. "We don't want any of this cargo loose in one of those damned hurricanes."

On the last day of May, Matthew announced impatiently, "Enough cargo. Let's go."

But Dresser coaxed two extra days out of him to squeeze the two last wagon loads below.

On the 4th of June, Matthew said goodbye quietly to a tearful and brave Martha. A small coterie of merchants, who had entrusted their goods to Dresser, stood on the pier-side looking anxiously at the ship as Matthew eased her skillfully out into the channel with a gentle off-pier breeze. Dresser Linthicum stood at his side, already trying to learn all he could about handling larger ships.

Matthew glanced at the eager young face next to him. "Are you learning anything?"

"Oh yes, Captain. I think I'm an expert in handling small craft. Never lost a race. As a matter of fact, both of your lieutenants, Jensen and MacClaren, used to race against me. They are good sailors and fine young men."

Matthew laughed. "Yes, young is the key word. They are as young as you are."

Dresser frowned. "Are we all too young?"

"Not too young. Just inexperienced. The boatswain and Jarrell and the gunner will make up for it. That's why I chose them. The boatswain, gunner, and I will have to stand watch with all of you until I can qualify you."

Linthicum grinned. "You'll let me stand watch by myself fairly soon?"

"Certainly. I figure in about two days."

Matthew looked up at the large sails rigged to the fore and main masts and asked Dresser, "For instance, what do you see up there?"

Linthicum looked up. "Both are luffing lightly. I knew that before I looked up because I could hear the edges of the sails fluttering."

"And what should I do?"

"Ease your helm until the fluttering stops."

"How much?"

"Try a point, sir."

"Good recommendation, although we could get by with a half a point if we were in danger." Matthew turned to the young sailor at the wheel. "One point to starboard."

The young man, an experienced sailor from the eastern shore, answered immediately, "One point to starboard, sir."

He spun the wheel sharply, and the ship responded quickly. The fluttering of the leading edge of the sails stopped. The man at the helm said, "Steady on south by southeast, sir."

Matthew smiled at Dresser, "You'll do. You stand the next watch with me tonight. Tomorrow you'll take the watch and I'll stand by. The next day you'll be alone. Lieutenant Jarrell and the gunner will qualify MacClaren and Jensen."

Linthicum grinned, "Then you'll get some sleep."

"Not much. A good captain never sleeps much at sea. I'll be on deck most of the night, but I'll sleep some in the daytime."

Linthicum was somber. "I like going to sea all right, but being a captain is a little too demanding for me. I think I'm more comfortable as a merchant ashore."

"We're all different, and our country needs all of us. I know I need you. We'll get along fine, and we'll come home rich if we're lucky."

"Lucky?"

"No, not really. Luck is just being a few seconds ahead of your opponent. I learned that from John Paul Jones."

Linthicum nodded soberly. I'll bet on you, and I hope to learn as much from you as you did from Captain Jones."

Chapter 9

For the rest of the first day, the *Mary* ran under full sail before a steady fifteen knot wind from the northwest. Linthicum, eagerly watching the quartermaster cast the log, noted that the ship was making a full twelve knots. He watched the captain enter the amount of "day's run" on the chart.

Dresser spoke up, "Captain, I estimate you're going to pass out of the Chesapeake Bay at night."

Matthew answered, "Yes, Dresser, I've done it before. If, this time, there are any French privateers patrolling the bay entrance, they'll never catch us at night. The entrance is too wide, and we are too fast. I trust you are capable of navigating at night, both on soundings and off shore."

"I can take and work out star sights at dawn and at dusk."

"And on soundings?"

"Oh, yes sir. I navigated my own boat all over the bay, and I've also taken it out to sea and up to the Delaware Bay. I learned to use a sextant and work out my sights and plot them on the chart. I'm ready to take over from you on the watch in this respect, too."

"I think you are well ahead of Jensen and MacClaren in navigation. Lieutenant Jarrell is a little ahead of you. On the way back I'll hold navigation school."

"I'm ready for anything, and the more I learn the more I like it."

Matthew laughed. "You'll take over the next watch. Now let's talk a little about the cargo below and what we're going to do with it."

Linthicum explained, "We have a hundred different items, all chosen to appeal to the needs and desires of the Spanish and particularly to the Cubans. Most are products from Maryland farms and manufacturing concerns. Some come from Philadelphia but most are from Baltimore's factories and stores. I knew you wanted to go to a Spanish dominated port."

"Certainly. Going to a British or French port would have been too dangerous. They might have tried to confiscate our cargo and even take over our ship. French privateers patrolling off their ports would have tried to capture us."

"Even if we enter a Spanish port?" asked Dresser.

"Yes. We'll have to avoid one or more French privateers lying off any Spanish port."

"Then American ships aren't really safe anywhere."

"Right," Matthew replied. "The French have been ignoring the international laws completely. I have lost count of the number of merchant ships they have taken."

Linthicum bristled. "But can't our government take any action against them?"

"No. The Congress passes resolutions against them, and the President castigates their government." Linthicum shrugged and drew several sheets of paper out of his shirt. "Here's the manifest."

Matthew scanned them carefully, stopped at several items and asked questions. When he had finished he handed the list back to Linthicum. "Looks fine. Now let's talk about loading cargo for the trip home."

"Havana doesn't have much we want. We'll have to move to another Cuban port where they gather products of their limited economy. I made some preliminary arrangements to go to Matanzas, a gathering and marketplace. The roads in Cuba are horrible. Most of what is available in Matanzas and the nearby countryside is tobacco, sugar cane, and the products of sugar cane, such as sugar and rum. They also market good mahogany."

Matthew sighed. "That's at least a sailing day away, depending on the wind. We'll have to keep track of French privateers off both ports and probably have to maneuver to avoid them."

Linthicum had taken in about all he could for one day, but he still did not want to go below. The sounds in the rigging and the sails intrigued him, and he walked the deck of the ship, listening to the various sounds and their changing pitches. As he reached the counter aft, he looked back at the endless succession of swells passing under the hull from the northwest. As they arrived, the ship heaved forward gently and then rolled to port. The slightly uneven motion made him sleepy. He took one last look at the bright Polaris star lying fixedly to the north and went below. As his head passed below in to the hatch, he realized how much he liked going to sea, and that life ashore as a merchant would never completely satisfy him.

For seven days the *Mary* made steady progress toward Cuba, with good weather and favorable wind. Matthew carefully avoided sails they sighted by using his superior speed and maneuvering ability to circle around them. Early on the morning of the seventh day, lookouts reported land ahead.

Jensen, who had the watch, checked the appearance of the peaks ahead against the charts. "Captain, we're on course for Havana. I make our time of arrival about noon if the wind holds."

Matthew checked the plot on the chart. "I agree. Notify the first lieutenant and boatswain and direct them to make all preparations for entering port. We'll have to anchor until I can make arrangements to sell and unload our cargo, either by barge or alongside a pier."

Matthew tried to memorize the various peaks and valleys. The hills were a brilliant green, completely covered with vegetation, and patches of tall trees were surrounded by cleared areas. Some were obviously planted with sugar cane waving in the breeze and others appeared to be clumps of bushes. The brilliant sun reflected the morning rain, still on the leaves, making the stretches of vegetation look like patches of diamonds.

Matthew turned his attention away from the beautiful sight and began to watch the crew making preparations for entering port. The noise and bustle on the decks awakened Linthicum who came topside soon, studying the land ahead.

Matthew watched him with growing affection. "Get some breakfast. You and I will be busy all day. Lieutenant Jarrell will be able to hold the fort."

Linthicum grinned and went below quickly. In half an hour he had breakfasted, shaved, and washed up, and was back on the quarterdeck.

With the port ahead still ten miles off, a lookout yelled down. "Sail ho, sir."

Matthew shook his head. "Our approach has been too slow and too late. Can you make her out?"

"Three masted frigate. No colors showing, sir."

Matthew shrugged. "French privateer for sure. We'll have to draw her off and sneak in at night."

Matthew turned to Boatswain Bostwick, who had the watch, "Boatswain. Bring her to east. Make maximum speed."

The boatswain gave the necessary orders and soon the *Mary* was sailing due east along the coast of Cuba.

The other ship piled on all canvas and turned to try to close the Mary but she fell astern slowly. Matthew turned to the boatswain, "Slow her so the Frenchman can close us from astern."

The boatswain reefed the mainsail and took in the jib. Those moves could not be seen easily by the frigate.

"Gunner, prepare to give her a couple of salvos of balls and then a dose of Baltimore grape."

Linthicum looked puzzled. "Sir, what's that?"

Matthew laughed. "It's really just a bag of iron balls that I get from a firm in Baltimore, although I can get it anywhere. It's called grape because the small balls look like grapes."

Linthicum nodded. "I see, but won't they shoot at us?"

"Certainly, but we'll shoot better and farther than they can with their inferior French guns, and after we've bloodied her nose, we'll draw away at our leisure."

In the meantime the crews of all four stern chasers were casting loose their guns and bringing up powder, balls, and sacks of grape. The gunner bustled about, making sure all was ready, occasionally lapsing into Spanish in his excitement. When he was satisfied, he touched his forelock and said, "Ready to fire, Captain."

"Very well. Load all four guns with balls. I plan to fire the two stern guns first and then veer to each side so you can fire the other two guns. When we're sure we're hitting, we'll shift to grape."

"Aye aye, sir." The gunner returned to his guns and gave the gun captains their instructions.

Matthew advised Linthicum, "Watch the gunner carefully. You'll probably be a battery commander someday, and he's an expert."

The French frigate drew closer, now dead astern. Her captain evidently thought his ship was the faster and certainly capable of outgunning his possible prey. Yet he fired his two bow chasers too soon and Linthicum held his breath. It was the first time he had been under fire, and he did not know what to expect. But soon he noted Matthew's calmness and he concentrated on watching the scene.

Two balls fell well astern. Matthew laughed. "Not even close, and I won't let him get much closer. We'll show him the range of our newer guns." He turned to Velasquez, "Gunner, fire when ready."

The gunner checked the lay of the guns and then turned to his crews. He ordered, "Guns three and four fire!"

The two guns pointing directly aft roared almost simultaneously. The wind, slightly on the quarter, carried the smoke away, and Linthicum could see one shot fall just forward of the oncoming ship's bow. "I only see one splash," he said excitedly.

Matthew agreed, "Right. The other one landed on their forecastle. It also means the captain and his crew will soon have grapes for breakfast."

Matthew turned to Bostwick. "Boatswain, veer two

points to port. As soon as the port gun has fired, come back four points to starboard."

"Aye aye, sir," the boatswain replied, and the ship began to swing. When the ship was steady the gunner fired the gun on that side. The boatswain immediately swung the ship again, and the fourth gun belched smoke and the last ball.

Matthew instructed Velasquez, "Now load grape in all guns."

Velasquez fired the stern guns as soon as the ship was steady," and then the boatswain and the gunner repeated the veer maneuver. The grape seemed to pepper the Frenchman, leaving small holes in the ship's sails. Matthew laughed. "You can imagine what's happening to the crew topside."

After two more salvos, Matthew seemed to grow tired of the havoc he was causing astern. "Enough breakfast for that hungry bastard. Now feed her a farewell salvo of solid balls."

After the last salvo appeared to hit 'midship, Matthew raised his hand. "Cease firing and increase speed to maximum. Let's leave her in our wake."

Dresser felt increasingly secure. Now he knew that they could challenge any ship, no matter how large it was, as long as they could bring it astern. Even much larger ships had no more bow chasers than they had stern chasers. He could see the wisdom in building a ship like the *Mary*.

Matthew turned to Valasquez. "Gunner, secure your guns but keep them ready for more action tonight."

Linthicum said, "But he's given up on us."

Matthew nodded. "The French bastard will go back to Havana, but he will try to catch us tonight."

After the Frenchman was out of sight, Matthew reversed course and headed for Havana Harbor.

He looked at Dresser and grinned. "Enough action?"

Dresser grinned back. "Oh, no sir. I'm ready for all you can find."

"We'll find a lot of action whenever we go where the commerce starts or ends."

Dresser said, "Exactly. That's where the products are. It's where we have to go to get them and where they will sell."

Matthew agreed, "And the French are no fools. They will know where to go to intercept our efforts to trade."

"Oh yes. Our problem will be to get by them in order to get into and out of ports without being taken."

"And you think we can do it?"

Matthew shrugged. "You'll find out tonight, and the event will show whether we can survive or not."

"I'm betting on you."

"So would I. I'd never bet on a Frenchie and not even on an Englishman if it comes to that again."

"But what will you do tonight?"

Matthew said, "I can't tell you exactly, but you will see soon."

Chapter 10

About 4 a.m., just before dawn, the lookout shouted, "Sail ho! The French Frigate is on our starboard bow!"

Matthew hauled the brass long glass out of the wooden cupboard and focused it on the looming ship. In the faint light of early dawn, he could make her out dimly. "The lazy bums are asleep! She's headed north under minimum canvas. Her starboard broadside is toward us, and the guns aren't even run out! Boatswain, come to port and head toward the harbor entrance. We'll sneak behind her and give her a sting in her tail as we go by."

The *Mary's* crew had had breakfast, then loaded and run out their guns just after midnight. Since that time they had lain down beside their guns awaiting a call. When the lookouts shouted, the gunners were on their feet almost immediately and in seconds were fully ready. Matthew passed the word to his officers. "Keep your guns laid on the Frenchman so you can fire immediately when I give the order."

In the growing light, the *Mary's* crew laid the starboard quarter chasers on the stern of the French frigate as best they could. As soon as there was enough light for the crews to aim the guns accurately, Matthew ordered, "Come to port and commence firing!"

The twin explosions shattered the early quietness of the dawn, and both shots landed on the decks of the frigate. Matthew shook his head as the Frenchmen came boiling up from the hatches and scurried about the decks of the frigate. He announced, "They'll give us no trouble! We'll be in port before they can come about and chase us!"

Linthicum said. "I'm beginning to understand this business of gunnery. No splashes sighted means both of the balls landed aboard."

Matthew nodded and turned to Velasquez. "Give them a

salvo of grape for their breakfast before we get out of range."

The French frigate was still headed north, trailing smoke as she dropped out of sight in the early morning mists."

Jarrell laughed. "Those Frenchmen are very peculiar. They will fight well when aroused about some point of honor, but when denied sleep or breakfast, they don't fight very well. The British were better. They fight because their officers make them and they have no alternative."

Matthew said, "I'm all for the American style. We fight well, and honor and officer's orders are not required."

Jarrell nodded in agreement. "I'm glad I'm an American. We'll get better in every respect as our country grows older and wiser."

"True, but our crews also fight better for money."

"Maybe so, but they fight for money and love of their country."

"Yes, their country represents liberty, freedom, and the principles for which the Revolutionary War was fought. This can be a powerful nation."

Matthew walked aft, thinking how the battle had just proven the extended range and reliability of their new guns. He walked by one of the guns and patted its pommel affectionately, whispering, "Great job." Then he had another thought. He would have to send word to Joshua Humphreys as soon as possible, informing him of the name and location of the gunsmith who had made their guns. Four hundred yards added range and improved reliability would make the guns to be installed on the six new frigates unbeatable. He grinned and patted another of the guns. "You've solved our country's and our own problem," he said. "You'll make us rich again."

Now Matthew concentrated on the *Mary* into a strange port. He could see the navigational markers on the headlands, matching those on the charts Linthicum had gotten from the Spanish embassy. The charts indicated adequate water between the buoys marking the entrance to the channel, and inside there was suitable water for anchoring just off the small pier shown. Matthew followed the middle of the channel slowly, although no other ship was in sight. "We'll go right in at good speed," Matthew announced.

By 9 a.m. he could see a pier jutting out from a warehouse and dropped anchor just off the end of the pier. "Boatswain, please put a boat in the water and give me four oarsmen and a coxswain to take me ashore."

In a few moments the boat was in the water. "Boat's alongside, captain," the boatswain reported.

Matthew turned to Linthicum. "Let's go, Dresser."

As he climbed over the bulwark, Matthew said to Lieutenant Jarrell, "You're in command, Lieutenant, until I return."

Ashore at a boat landing, Matthew and Dresser climbed up a brow and walked to an office in the shore side of the building. Matthew knocked at a door under a large sign proclaiming, "Castro y Hijos," and they went in. The pair were met by a smiling Cuban standing just inside the door. The Cuban removed his cigar. "Buenos dias, señores."

Castro was of medium height. He sported the usual Cuban mustache and wore his sideburns a little longer than usual. He was very handsome, and Matthew thought he must cut quite a swath amongst the ladies in Havana.

Matthew held out his hand and grinned. "Captain Matthew Christopher, of the American merchantman *Mary*. Do you speak English?"

The Cuban smiled. "Oh, yes. I am Juan Castro, owner of the Castro Export-Import business with headquarters here. Please come in and sit down."

Matthew and Dresser followed him into the inner office, vacant and large and opulent. Large over-stuffed chairs were grouped in the middle of the room in front of a mammoth mahogany desk. Pictures covered the walls, and Matthew was sure most of them were expensive originals.

Castro noted Matthew's interest. "Like it?" he asked.

"Very much. It makes mine look like a barn."

"Yes, that's the way I started. Now I've come a long way and I hope to stay here. Please take a chair and let's get started on our business."

Matthew presented Dresser to Castro. "Lieutenant Linthicum, who is also head of the Linthicum Export-Import business.

Castro shook Linthicum's hand. "I hope to see much of you in the future." Then he smiled warmly and said, "Welcome, gentlemen. Now how can we do business?"

Matthew explained, "I'd like to do all my trading in your port officially and sell all my cargo to you or to other parties here endorsed by you. My government recommends that I do this and of course I will follow their guidance."

Castro laughed. "I run this port and this town. You are welcome today and any other time you wish to visit here. "May I see your manifests?"

After Castro read through the long lists of goods, he said, "I think I'd like to take all of it. As a matter of fact, you are in the only location in Cuba where it can be unloaded from your ship."

Matthew said, "That sounds good to me. Can Linthicum make arrangements with you for buying and loading outgoing cargo?"

Castro smirked. "If it's mahogany, sugar, molasses, coffee, or hennequen. That's all we have for sale in Cuba, but, you can't load it here. You'll have to move to Matanzas, a small port about 50 miles east of here."

"Couldn't cargo be brought here?"

Castro smiled amusedly. "You haven't seen our roads yet. You have to go where products are grown and harvested. Señor Linthicum will have to go overland by horse and make arrangements for it. I'll send four armed men with him to ensure his safety."

"Will he be in danger of being harmed or taken into custody by French forces?"

Castro laughed and flicked the ash off his long cigar. "They wouldn't dare come ashore. There are Spanish banditos every mile along the coast."

"Are they dangerous?"

"Very, but they only rob each other."

"And your four men are capable of taking care of my man?"

"Not by themselves. They will wear the uniform of my private militia, and the banditos wouldn't dare bother them. If they did they know they would be caught and hanged."

"I feel better about Lieutenant Linthicum," Matthew said, glancing at Dresser. "But I'll have to sail around the French frigate to get there just as I did to get in here."

Castro smiled knowingly. "They have many spies here. However, I'd bet on you. Your ship looks trim and speedy. I watched you come in past the frigate through the windows. You were very clever and you had no trouble."

Matthew nodded. "Thank you. I take it we have an agreement. Can I go back to my ship and move it alongside?"

"Oh, yes. I look forward to many deals with you. Will you join my wife and me at dinner tonight? We can settle some of the details."

"Of course. I would be honored. Will you tell me how to reach your house?"

Castro answered, "My aids will pick you up in my carriage at 7 p.m. at the landing. My house is the big white one back in the hills."

"My god! I thought that was a king's castle. It's very imposing."

Castro laughed and modestly de-ashed his cigar. "Well, I'm the closest thing to a king around here."

Chapter 11

Matthew went back to the *Mary*, swinging to her anchor near the pier where the officers were eagerly waiting. They were lined up leaning on the bulwark near the gangway.

Jensen asked, "What's the news, Captain? Was Castro what you were looking for?"

Matthew grinned. "Patience! I think so. We get underway immediately and go alongside that pier over there. Then we unload cargo as fast as we can."

The boatswain frowned. "How, sir?"

"The pier has two cranes. Not too big, but they'll do. There will be a lot of Cuban stevedores coming aboard. The trick will be to keep them at work and not let them steal us blind. They're pretty bad."

The gunner smiled broadly. "I've had lots of experience with men like that. We'll have plenty of armed sentries, and I'll watch them personally."

The boatswain scratched his chin, still unshaven since his early morning duties. "We could rig spars I have below and attach them to the main booms to help bring up cargo from the holds below."

"Good. Get at it as soon as we are alongside. We want to get unloaded as soon as possible and go to another port to reload. Now let's get underway," urged Matthew.

Jensen asked thoughtfully, "Why are you so concerned, captain?"

"That damned Frenchman worries me. He might even send for reinforcements."

"Now, captain, that's not probable. Just calm down. We'll be all right with only one opponent out there."

"I guess you're right. I just don't expect to find another Frenchman as dumb as this one."

After the *Mary* slid alongside the pier, a large group of

stevedores appeared and swarmed aboard. Velasquez grinned and posted his sentries. He tried to keep the stevedores topside as long as possible, and when it became necessary to send them below he kept men watching them to make sure they didn't put objects under their shirts.

Matthew grew tired of watching the unloading operations and sighed. "Lieutenant Jensen, take charge. Linthicum has to go to a port 50 miles down the coast, and I've got to go have dinner with Señor Castro."

Suddenly a carriage drove up and skidded to a stop. Liveried men jumped down and stood at attention. Matthew sighed again. "I'm leaving as soon as I can bathe and change."

Jensen laughed. "I wouldn't want to change jobs with you or Linthicum tonight."

Before Matthew left for Castro's home, a group of four armed Cuban soldiers rode up, guiding a saddled horse. They wore bandoliers of ammunition and carried rifles and pistols.

Matthew looked up and said to Jensen, "Send word to Linthicum."

Soon Linthicum dashed up on deck, sword at his side, a saddle bag thrown over one shoulder, and a cape thrown over the other. He ran down to the group of soldiers and saluted the man obviously in charge. There was a flurry of further salutes. Linthicum placed the saddle bag over the withers of the horse, threw back his cape, mounted the horse skillfully, and clattered off after the soldiers.

Matthew, watching him with awe, shook his head and said to Jensen, "That young man has class. He'll go a long way in this or any other business. Now take charge. I'm leaving. Don't let anyone aboard without our armed sailors present."

Jensen nodded. "I understand. With regard to Linthicum, you're right. He has class. He also speaks Spanish. He told me he learned it in college because he thought he might need it someday, regardless of his occupation. He also speaks some French."

Matthew shrugged. "And I suppose you speak Swedish?"

Jensen laughed. "As a matter of fact I do, but so far it hasn't helped me much. I'm learning Spanish."

———————

Matthew walked over to the carriage, trying to show the same class displayed by Linthicum, but the steps were difficult and he stumbled slightly as he got in. He sat back on the stiff cushions. As the driver struggled to follow the ruts in the road leading to the distant house, Matthew tried to steal an occasional peek at the mansion on the hill. As they approached he could tell it was as big up close as he had suspected from a distance. It was huge. He could see that it was multi-storied with a veranda on all four sides. Bougainvillea covered all four sides, making the house appear to float in a sea of purple. A long driveway lined with trees led up to the entrance.

Matthew held tightly to the strap as they bounced over the ruts and holes. After twenty minutes, the carriage drew up to the large entrance under a portico.

Matthew got out, waved away the offered assistance of two liveried servants, and was met by a smiling Castro with his inevitable cigar.

"Welcome, Captain Christopher, to my humble domicilio."

Matthew looked around. "It isn't humble, but it's certainly beautiful."

Castro said, "From up here you can see why the rest of our roads are impassable except on horseback."

Castro escorted Matthew up a huge staircase and into a spacious sitting room. A woman seated in a large chair rose and came forward, extending her hand to Matthew. "Welcome, Captain," she said "My husband has told me a lot about you and your beautiful ship now swinging in the harbor."

Her hands were covered with jewelled rings as was her hair, which was put up using diamond clips. Matthew judged her gown was from Paris. Certainly it was the equal of any he had seen in Washington or Philadelphia. In the center of her finery was a beautiful, intelligent face. And he was instantly charmed.

Matthew took her hand, bent over it, and kissed it. "Madam, I am honored to meet you."

"My name is Eugenia Castro. My husband was ambassador to the President of the United States for four years. I enjoyed my life there, and I learned your language and customs. My chef will prepare some dishes he learned about in Washington, and he will also offer you a few Cuban delights. I hope you will enjoy them. Now please let me offer you a typical Cuban refreshment. A little rum and a lot of fruit juice added. Please take one and sit next to me."

Matthew sat down and enjoyed several Cuban rum drinks. After a fascinating conversation with his hostess, Matthew enjoyed a long and filling dinner of many exotic courses, mostly seafood.

Around midnight, Mrs. Castro rose. "Captain, please excuse me. I know you will want to talk business with my husband. I look forward to seeing you on future visits, and I hope you will join us for dinner frequently."

"Thank you, madam. Your dinner was excellent and I enjoyed learning more about your country. I, too, look forward to my return."

Mrs. Castro then left the men to discuss their business venture. Castro said, "Captain, let's go on my cool veranda, have a nice cigar, and some more rum punches. We can talk a little business. I feel you and I will do a lot of it in the future, for the possibilities are endless."

Matthew laughed. "I hope so. I expect to send you a shipload of cargo about once a month, and I hope to return with your products."

Castro nodded. "I am sure you recognize that I am the only man in Cuba who can take all of your cargo and assemble a return cargo for you. Also, I own the only bank that can deal with the United States banks on equal terms.

Business between us will be quite easy."

"Yes, Juan, if you will permit me to use that familiar name when we talk in private."

"Of course. I will also call you Matthew in private, but when others can hear I am sure you will agree we should use our formal names."

"Certainly. Now there is one item we have not covered. I do not know what you will pay me for my cargo or what you will charge me for the return cargo."

Castro shrugged. "I am well aware that you will make a lot of money as will I. I have almost a monopoly here."

"But what about the other Cubans, both rich and poor. Won't they object?"

"Certainly they may. If I treat them poorly they will rebel, but I expect to treat them fairly and still make a lot of money. I know my people well and they like me. They will let me alone. Trust me."

Matthew sighed. "Well, Juan, I must also trust you to set prices so we can all make money. Now I must go back to my ship and make sure unloading is going well."

Castro tapped his cigar and raised his eyebrows. "Caramba! Matthew, you have been at sea too long. Are you not interested in some of the Havana night life? It is very good, and I can take you anywhere safely."

"Thank you, but no. Now if I could borrow your carriage, please. I am very tired. I was up all night looking for that damned Frenchman. We didn't sleep much, but he did. That's why we had little trouble getting in."

"Of course. I will see you tomorrow morning. If all goes well, we will set a date for your move to Matanzas."

"Fine, Juan. I am eager to return to my country."

———

The unloading proceeded as expected, and after three days Matthew returned to Castro's office. Castro was seated behind his huge desk.

Matthew said, "Juan, I estimate I will be ready to go tomorrow night. Will Matanzas be ready?"

"Certainly. But how will you get past the privateer out there? He will know when you are going to sea, and he'll know you are headed for Matanzas."

Matthew shrugged. "I don't think that will make much difference. I will leave in the dark. He can't shoot at me at night. The French aren't good at it."

Castro smiled. "I'll count on you to win because I know you are superior in speed and seamanship. I'll try to help you to get into Matanzas. I'll arrange for two bonfires to be lit on the night you plan to arrive, marking the limits of safe water on both sides of the harbor. But you will need something else for your safety."

"Luck?"

Castro laughed. "That, too. But I will provide a navigational range marking the course you should take into the harbor. The front range on the beach will be a single bonfire. Just line it up with another behind it."

"And how will I know it?"

"My men will hold a blanket up in front of it for a few seconds every two minutes. The back part of the range will be two bonfires side by side, and they will be obscured the same way every four minutes."

"The whole arrangement will be perfect. I'll have no trouble."

Chapter 12

Two days later, the *Mary* was completely unloaded, and Matthew moved her from the pier to a convenient anchorage. He noticed the high waterline and the ship's uneasiness as it rolled from the swells coming in the harbor entrance, but he decided not to go through the futile process of ballasting just for the trip to Matanzas. Castro had predicted mild swells and since there were no indications of a storm, Matthew decided to take a chance for the short trip.

About midnight Matthew hoisted his anchor, made sail, and headed out the entrance. Jensen, who had the first watch, scanned the darkness anxiously looking for signs of the French frigate. Jensen called up to the lookouts, "Be alert up there. We want to see the French ship as far away as possible."

"Aye aye," came the answer.

Matthew nodded. "Your warning didn't do any harm, and it might have helped, but you can assume that those men are just as concerned as we are."

Jensen took a deep breath. "You're right, Captain, but I'm concerned about that bastard out there." Jensen began to pace up and down.

Matthew noted his nervous actions by the light in the binnacle and laughed. "Don't worry. He hasn't got enough guts to come in this close in the darkness. He'll wait offshore, hoping to pick us up in the daylight as we go down the coast to Matanzas."

"Will we?"

"Hell, no. We'll pass him in the night, go north for half a day, head east for half a day, then turn south for Matanzas. We'll enter the harbor well before dawn, when it's still dark and he's still asleep. He'll probably be off Matanzas by that time. The Frenchmen aren't worth much early in the morning, and we can count on him to be asleep then."

"But can we get into Matanzas in the dark?"

"Oh, yes. Señor Castro has arranged a set of bonfires to help us navigate safely. Should be easy. They will mark the limits of the harbor headlands, and the channel will be marked by range bonfires. It will be easy."

It was. The Frenchman had moved east, giving up on intercepting the *Mary* after her exit. She sat off the entrance to Matanzas, waiting patiently for the arrival of the *Mary*.

Matthew was confident that they could run past even if they knew he was coming. Accordingly, he let his crew sleep as long as possible before having them called at two a.m. After a full breakfast, they were in high spirits and hoping to get a shot at the "sleeping frog," as they called the ship.

About 3 a.m., under full sail, the *Mary* approached Matanzas on a southerly heading. The lookouts sighted the signal bonfires and reported them.

Jensen and the watch acknowledged the lookout's reports. "Well, I'll be damned! Getting in should be as easy as you said it would be," he marveled to Matthew.

The Frenchman was still a formidable obstacle, and Matthew, cautiously watching her movements, waited until she was on an easterly course. Then he changed their own course to pass under her stern. When he judged they were astern of the frigate, he headed directly for the range bonfires.

Suddenly a light became visible on the Frenchman's stern and was reported by the lookouts. Matthew looked at it carefully through his long glass. Suddenly he laughed. "It's the captain shaving and having an early breakfast. His steward forgot to close the after ports to his cabin. Velasquez, let him have the starboard guns. We'll interrupt his breakfast and wake up the whole ship."

Velasquez grinned. "I think we can see well enough with that bright light to aim the two guns, but after they go off the night vision of my gun crews will be destroyed. We won't be able to fire anymore."

Matthew laughed. "You won't have to. They can't see to fire at us at all, and in a few minutes we'll be in the safety of the harbor."

At least one of the balls hit, and consternation reigned on the decks of the Frenchman. Shouts could be heard plainly as the men on deck ran to their guns and tried to locate the *Mary* in the darkness.

The *Mary's* crew leaned on the starboard rail watching the spectacle. "Damnedest show I ever saw!" said Jensen.

"Sorry Linthicum missed it," said MacClaren. "Maybe he could have translated some of the French comments. That would have been first-class comedy."

Ashore, Linthicum was finishing his arrangements, and when the *Mary* glided in to anchor just after dawn, Linthicum was in a boat on the way out.

On the quarterdeck, he exclaimed, "Captain, what was that firing about early this morning? I thought they might have taken you."

"Not a chance. Now tell me what you have for us and how long it will take to load it."

"Three loaded barges will be here within the hour. I hope the boatswain can rig spars and main booms as he did before. We'll have to off-load the barges with stevedores and our crew. It will probably take about four days, but maybe we can make it in three with the boatswain's help."

Matthew sighed. "Good. I can use several days and nights of sleep."

The cargo was made up of sugar, butts of molasses, bales of hennequen to be made into American binder twine, coffee, cigars, and some fresh fruit for the crew. When it was all below and safely secured, a barge load of Cuban mahogany logs came aboard. Matthew was careful to secure the cargo well, mindful of the severe storms in the area.

The loading was completed on the morning of the fifth

day, and Matthew allowed the crew to sleep the rest of the afternoon. "I want them well-rested and sharp for our run out there tonight. The Frenchmen will be crazy to get at us, and they'll be close to Matanzas this time."

About midnight Matthew gave orders to get the ship underway, and the officers made their rounds rousing the crew and having them fed.

MacClaren was apprehensive as he took the first watch, but Matthew tried to calm him. "The off-shore wind will be at its maximum, and we'll go right by them. Don't worry about it. It will be my responsibility."

When he was sure they were clear of the left promontory, he ordered a course change to the left. He searched the area to sea, and then he could see the faint white loom of sails. It was the Frenchman.

Velasquez said, "Captain, I don't think we can see well enough to shoot in the darkness, and the moon won't come up until 2 a.m."

"Right, and he won't be able to shoot at us even if he sights us."

When the frigate was abeam, Matthew changed course to the north and ordered a course for Annapolis.

The loom of the French sails disappeared slowly to the south as Matthew ordered all sails set, and the *Mary* leaped ahead. Even Jensen relaxed.

Matthew asked, "Linthicum, what is the French word for goodbye?"

"Au revoir."

"Ah yes. That's close enough."

Linthicum laughed. "We won't have to stand on protocol. She doesn't even know we're gone."

Chapter 13

For two days the *Mary* ran north in good weather. On the evening of the second day, Matthew noted a change in the sky at dusk. The barometer began to drop slowly and swells grew from the east.

Velasquez came aft to the quarterdeck. "Sir, this isn't my business, but I don't like the weather. A hurricane may be forming to the east and moving northwest. Several signs exist that usually precede one."

Matthew nodded. "It is your business. Although you are the gunner, you are the most experienced seagoing officer I have. I agree with you, and you and I are the only ones aboard with enough experience to recognize the danger. I think the center is now due east. If we continue north at ten knots or more I hope we will pass safely ahead of it, unless it veers markedly to the north or northwest."

"I agree, but we'll still get some of the bad weather preceding the center of a hurricane."

Matthew said, "I'll take the watch. Tell Jarrell and the lieutenants to supervise the securing of the cargo with double lashings. Pay particular attention to the mahogany logs. Also, secure the equipment on deck such as the anchors. I'll continue to run at maximum speed as long as I can."

Velasquez left to carry out his orders, and soon the officers and crew scurried topside to begin the securing. The seamen yelled back and forth over the noise of the increasing winds as they passed the lines around the gear on deck.

About 8 p.m. Linthicum came on deck to take the watch. He examined the chart, and he noted the weather, the set and amount of the sails, and the readings of the barometer. Then he walked over to Matthew. "Sir, I'm ready to take over the watch, but I don't see the officer of the watch."

"I took over from Velasquez and sent him below to

inform the other officers about securing the ship."

"I didn't hear him. I must have been getting ready for my watch." Linthicum frowned. "I've never been in a hurricane before, but I've heard of the signs of one. I understand these are terrible storms, sometimes having winds of two-hundred miles an hour. I see the dropping barometer, the direction of the swells and the wind. How do you put this together?"

"Simple. The direction the swells are coming from indicates the present position of the storm's center. It is just a big circular whirlwind with a quiet center of about forty miles across. The whole thing moves from west to north, and its direction of movement usually changes slowly as it moves north. The barometer will drop steadily and the amount it drops indicates roughly the distance away from the center. At present the center of the storm is a little south of east. The winds in the storm flow counter-clockwise in this hemisphere. Now, as you would expect, the winds are from the northeast. Fortunately we can make maximum speed to the north with this wind direction. I would judge the center is about five hundred miles away."

"What about the speed and direction of the center's movement?"

"I can only guess. I think it will move northwest." Matthew shrugged. "This is always the unknown. The winds are now at thirty knots, and we can continue on our course for awhile longer without reefing. I think our speed is up to fifteen knots at this time. You can take charge of the watch now."

Linthicum frowned. "But, sir?"

Matthew laughed. "Don't worry. I'm not leaving the quarterdeck except to get my oil skins. I'll send some up for you and the rest of the watch. I'll tell you when to reef sails or change course as necessary. The more wind we can stand the faster we can get out of danger. At 35 knots of wind we'll take our first reef. At 45 we'll take a second, and we'll hope that will be the maximum."

"And at 55?"

Matthew shrugged. "We may have lost this bet, and we'll have to run under bare poles and maybe a sea anchor. Look at the barometer now, check it every ten minutes thereafter, and give me your readings. I'll be watching the direction of the swells and wind."

"Sir, the gunner told me about dangerous versus safe semicircles, but I don't think I followed him exactly since he was in a hurry. Can you explain it better than he did?"

"Well, you know these storms are rotating masses of air around a center of calmness. The winds usually average about 60 miles an hour but have been known to reach two-hundred. This would be a disaster, but hopefully you and I will never see it. And you already know I estimate the whole system is moving at about 30 miles an hour between west and northwest."

"Ah, I understand. The winds in the north side have the speed of rotation plus the speed of translation over the surface added to them. The wind on the other side has the speed of translation subtracted from them, so that is the safer area."

"You've got it. The north side is the dangerous semicircle with winds as much as 60 knots higher than the winds in the safe semicircle."

"Then why are we headed north through the dangerous senmicircle?"

"I am taking a chance. If we turned and headed south, we might be able to pass the hurricane to its south in much less winds. But on the other hand, the storm might change direction to the southwest, and we might be caught between it and the weather shore of Cuba. That would be a disaster. If we can get across the path of the hurricane, we will avoid a lot of trouble and save a lot of time. But don't assume my decision is one you should follow in the future. Ordinarily it is better to go to the safe semicircle if you have enough time and no enemy around to take into account."

Linthicum shuddered. "I'm glad you are making this decision. I'm even more convinced that I was suited to be a merchant."

Matthew grinned. "But then there's always inflation and bankruptcy."

"Yes, but I won't drown in them."

"Certainly not, but trust me. I have a flair for guessing the weather, and I predict this storm will slow to 20 knots and continue on northwest until we pass it. Not all ships have our speed and maneuverability."

For two hours Linthicum paced the quarterdeck nervously. Soon the rain started. He began consulting the barometer every ten minutes and reporting to the Captain. The rain intensified, and initially Linthicum was glad the captain had sent below for the oil skins, but water continued to seep down his neck. The rain remained heavy, but it soon steadied, and the winds did slow somewhat, although Linthicum still didn't like them.

For the next few hours, Matthew paced the quarterdeck, usually a calm and private area. The quarterdeck, even on merchant ships, was forbidden to anyone but the captain, the officer of the watch, the quartermaster of the watch, and the helmsman. All others avoided the area so that those on watch could concentrate on their duties.

Matthew moved forward of the quarterdeck and leaned on the bulwark, listening to the wave patterns hitting the hull and noticing the changes in them. At the same time he could hear the standing rigging beside him from the bulwark up to the masts straining and thrumming. The frequency changed slightly as the ship rolled. Further behind him the operating rigging also thrummed, and the frequencies differed depending on how tight the particular crewmen had secured the sheets and halliards.

Then Matthew noticed two crewmen on watch who had sauntered over to lean on the bulwark next to him. Unlike the quarterdeck, this was a common area, and Matthew frequently went to it so he could talk to the crew freely.

One of the men lifted his hand and touched his hairline

with a finger. It was a form of salute. Matthew raised his hand in a similar gesture. "Captain. May we ask you a question?" one man asked.

"Certainly. Any time."

"Why did you try to cross ahead of the storm?"

"I took a chance, and as you see, it paid off. You'll get home a week earlier than you would have if I'd gone south around it."

The sailor grinned and looked at his companion. "See, I told you he was doing the right thing."

The second man shrugged. "He always does."

They raised their hands in another salute. The first man said, "Thank you, Captain, sleep well if you ever get below."

Matthew nodded. "Thank you. Maybe tomorrow."

By midnight the barometer steadied at 29.00. "Good sign," the captain said. "We're gaining on it. The swells are now fifteen degrees off the stern."

But the wind still rose and at thirty-five knots the Captain ordered the first reef taken. "Call the boatswain!" he commanded.

Soon the boatswain climbed up to the deck and looked around. "Damn!" he said. "This doesn't look good!"

Matthew shouted over the wind, "Not too bad. For four hours running under a lot of sail we're 60 miles more to the north. In another four hours, even reefed, we'll be 120 miles north of the storm center. By dawn we may be completely out of the dangerous area."

The *Mary* had rolled to port 30 degrees as the long swells passed under her counter, but the rolling eased as the swells began to come from astern. Linthicum felt the need to heave over the lee rail, but he swallowed hard and tried to keep his mind occupied by recounting the inventory of their cargo. The feeling soon eased, and he felt better.

At 4 a.m. Velasquez came to the quarterdeck to take over

the watch. Linthicum reported his relief to the captain and started below.

"Just a minute," said Matthew. "Don't you want to stay up here and see how this comes out?"

Linthicum paled slightly, but said, "Yes, sir. I'll be back in 15 minutes."

Matthew grinned, "Try to remember to get rid of everything over the lee side."

When Linthicum returned his face was still a little pale.

The captain grinned. "You look better. By daylight you can get a good look at the swells, the wind, and the barometer and probably go below. I think we've passed the danger now, or will soon pass it."

By 8 a.m., when Jensen came to the quarterdeck to relieve the watch, Matthew stretched his muscles. "What do you think, Jensen?"

"Well, sir, the direction of the swells is now on the port quarter. The barometer is going up slowly, and the wind is now down to 25 knots and from the southeast. That should mean that the storm center is now about 200 miles to the southwest and we're past it."

"Right. The wind will lessen gradually and the rain will stop about noon. By mid afternoon we may see some sun."

Linthicum shook his head. "I don't think I'll be here to see it. I have to go below now to get some sleep before my next watch."

Matthew smiled. "Sailors don't need sleep. I think I'll stay up here."

Linthicum sighed. "I'm meant to be a merchant, and they can sleep as long as the store is closed."

"You'll be busy when we get in."

"Oh, yes. That's my time to stay up late selling our goods. I can take that."

The next four days were increasingly clear, and most of

the French privateers were still sheltering somewhere, await-ing the storm's passage. At noon on day seven of the return voyage, the entrance to Chesapeake Bay loomed ahead. Matthew had deliberately given Cape Hatteras a wide berth because of the treacherous weather off the cape, and as a precaution against a privateer taking station off the busy pas-sage area, looking for a stray ship.

The waters were clear of danger, and they soon passed Cape Charles. Matthew watched the shape of the cape as it slid by. He noticed its difference from the brilliant green of Cuba's coastline. The water was different, too. Cuba's bright blue was now the dull green of the bay entrance.

That evening and well into the night the crew worked hard to ready the ship to enter port. The captain and Linthicum walked about watching the crew. Up forward they came across Velasquez and a small group of gun cap-tains working on a gun.

Linthicum was curious. "Exactly what are you doing?"

"First, we're unloading it. Then we'll clean and inspect it."

"You mean the gun was loaded all during the storm?" Linthicum asked.

The next morning the spires of Annapolis churches were sighted at the head of the Severn River. Matthew took the *Mary* up to the river's entrance of the Severn river, and maneuvered the ship alongside a pier at the Christopher shipyard fitting out area.

Eric and Martha were on the pier as the ship eased gently alongside. Eric bounded aboard in spite of his arthritis, but Martha stayed on the pier.

Eric shouted even before he reached the top of the hasti-ly placed brow. "Did you do well?"

Matthew replied, "Oh, yes. I'll leave Dresser to tell you the details. I'm going ashore to greet my wife. I'll see you in the shipyard office tomorrow morning."

At the bottom of the brow, Matthew took Martha in his arms and kissed her deeply. After a minute, she pushed him away gently, rearranged her hair, staightened her hat, and grinned. "Enough, sailor. Let's go home."

The following morning Eric was in the office at dawn, pacing up and down, muttering to himself. "Damned young whippersnapper! Dresser would only give me a minute yesterday. He insisted on going home right away to see his wife! He's almost as bad as Matthew."

By 7 a.m., when Elizabeth Buchanan arrived at the office, Eric had partially calmed down. Elizabeth asked, "How was the voyage?"

Eric groaned. "Good, I think. Dresser will be down here soon with the manifests for us. What's more important, Matthew is going to get here soon, if he ever gets out of bed, and tell us something he said was very important."

Elizabeth asked, "What is it?"

"He didn't say. He was in too much of a hurry to kiss his wife and go home."

"He certainly was, and can't you guess what he's going to tell you?"

"Maybe he thinks Martha is pregnant."

Elizabeth laughed. "You're the eternal optimist. It isn't that."

"Well, what?"

"He's going to tell you he plans to convert the *Mary* to a privateer."

"Well, why couldn't he tell me that last night?"

"Because you're an unsentimental old man."

"So?"

"He wanted to tell Martha first, so he could get her permission to go to sea as a privateer captain on the *Mary*."

Chapter 14

At 8 a.m., after Elizabeth had been pacing for an hour, she could stand no more, and she looked out the front window facing the street. Then she gasped, put her hand over her mouth, and ran out the door.

Eric quickly put down his coffee cup and yelled after Elizabeth's fast-retreating form, "You run too fast. You might break a leg. What's wrong?"

She didn't answer, so Eric ran out as fast as his legs would carry him. Elizabeth was running toward a bewildered Matthew, standing in the middle of the street just in front of two snorting and stamping horses. The irate driver of the carriage swore and honked his bulb horn again. "Dammit, man, are you still asleep?"

Matthew raised his hand in a gesture of pacification and grinned at the driver. "My deepest apologies to you, sir, and to your magnificent horses. I guess I was still sleeping." Matthew stepped aside and raised his hat.

The driver, angry, but cooling down rapidly in response to Matthew's grin, shook his reins at the horses, raised his hat in return, and drove off.

Elizabeth was frantic to get to Matthew. "Are you all right?"

Matthew laughed. "Oh, yes, I have a lot on my mind, and I was concentrating on what I was to tell you folks this morning."

Eric clomped over as fast as he could. "My God, boy, come out of the street and inside where it's safe. This is a dangerous place out here with all these crazed drivers dashing about."

Elizabeth frowned. "Eric, he wasn't any worse than you are as a driver."

Eric shrugged. "Never mind that. Matthew, come inside and relieve our anxiety."

Elizabeth shook her head and explained to Matthew, "It's been a six-coffee morning for your father already. I'm about to run out of coffee, and even the supply of tea is low."

———•———

When he was firmly in place behind the big desk in the drafting room, Matthew said to Elizabeth, "Bring in John Paul, Ryan and you two, and we'll get to this."

While they were waiting for the group to gather, Eric said, "Martha must have given you a tough night."

Matthew raised his eyebrows. "I don't know what you're talking about. The first few hours after a sailor gets home are never tough. They are wonderful."

"Well?"

"All right, I'll admit that the first morning at breakfast was tough."

"And you told her then?" asked Eric.

"Told her what?"

"All of the changes we want to make."

"Yes. All of them. I never keep anything from Martha."

"I'm sure she wept a lot."

Matthew sighed. "Yes. There were some tears at first, but you know Martha. In the end she wiped them away and told me I could go ahead."

"She was too easy on you." Eric determined.

"Well, she did remind me that we have five children now, she doesn't want any more, and I am not as necessary now. She said she could do without me."

"I take it she was pulling your leg?"

"I hope so. We'll find out."

———•———

Eric said, "Now let's make this official. Everyone is here. What do we do and when do we do it? Here it is, August, 1797, and the French are getting worse." He pointed to a newspaper laying on the table. "They are getting bolder every day."

"I know" said Matthew. "I saw them in action in the Caribbean against us, and I itch to capture or destroy some of them, particularly one off Havana waiting for our next ship. We were lucky to get away."

Eric stood up and shouted, "Now you are ready to go at it!"

Matthew stood up too, and raised a cup of coffee. "To the *Mary!* She'll do it for us."

Eric raised his cup. "Great!" They lowered their cups and Eric continued, "We've been ready to do this for months. The real question is do we convert a second ship?"

"Certainly. As soon as the *Martha* gets back from her trip to Havana, we'll have our other shipyard in Chestertown start on her. The ships we have on the ways will be ready to take over the merchant mission soon. We should speed up their completion as much as possible."

Eric nodded. "I'll start our shipyard on the conversion immediately. The plans are on the drafting table, but we have to be careful to integrate all of these plans."

"I don't follow you."

"I mean the return of funds from a privateer will be ten times as much as those from a merchantman."

"I understand. I'll make sure it comes out that way. We need all the money we can get." Matthew continued, "But there's another matter. The *United States* will be commissioned in July of this year, and she'll go into service the following year. Captain Barry sent a letter to Bruce asking him to report in May of next year. He'll just be out of school then. That'll meet Martha's last objection."

Eric's eyebrows shot up. "You mean you arranged all this last night?"

"Not all of it. Needless to say, I didn't sleep much, but I didn't need to. I've been working on it for months. Now we can get back to the conversion of the *Mary*. There are hundreds of thousands of dollars in prizes waiting for us. As you know, we will be in danger of losing our shipyards soon if we can't pump some cash into them. The last years of poor times have eaten into our capital piled up from during the Revolutionary War, and we have been using it too rapidly."

Eric sighed. "Yes, I know. Inflation and labor costs have eaten into my wife's farm the same way. The Linthicums put up a good pretense, but they're hurting too. Every day counts. Now tell me just how do you want the *Mary* changed."

"Just make her over as we put into her original plans. I want twelve 20-pounders for her broadside. Add four bow chasers. Don't forget to be extra cautious when you convert the forward magazine."

"I understand why you feel that way."

"How long will it take to do all of this?"

"Until about August of 1798."

"Just time enough to see Bruce off to sea."

"Just about."

"What about the anticipated legislation to seize foreign ships?"

"Joshua Humphreys sent me a letter predicting that in early July 1798, Congress would authorize the sale of captured enemy ships, and that most of the proceeds would go to the captain, crew, and owners of the privateers. This sounds hopeful, but no one can predict whether or not the Congress will do anything and certainly not when."

Matthew stood and paced around the room. "That will be close. We'll have to find some legal loopholes to take care of us until the legislation actually passes. Maybe our lawyer can come up with something."

"No, we have to keep this to ourselves and do what we want to do," Eric said.

"Right. Now what else?"

"You'll need more officers and men. The *Mary* will no longer be just a cargo carrier. All the extra guns and prize crews will require more officers and men."

"The numbers of fine young men available won't decrease. I've got a list of volunteers a yard long. The officers will be a more difficult matter."

"What about captains?"

Matthew said, "Scotty MacIntosh will take the second

ship when she's converted. I'll let Jensen take one of the merchant ships. He'll get some more experience before he's needed. Then I'll bring him back to take over the *Mary*. Better yet, I think Jarrell will make the best captain of all our officers."

"And Jarrell wants to stay at sea?" asked Eric.

"Oh, yes. For many reasons."

"You'll let the *Mary* go?"

"I promised Martha. The day isn't far off."

"I don't believe it."

Matthew sighed. "Be patient. I figure one voyage on the *Mary* after her conversion. That should add several million dollars in prize money."

"It certainly is more rewarding than just running merchant ships around."

"It is, but we'll have to revert to that means later. We have to take advantage of the French while they permit it and the law allows."

"I know you want to command the *Mary* just because you want to go to sea on her. But there's something else driving you, isn't there?"

Matthew nodded. "Yes, there is. I want to go to the Caribbean and take that cheeky French frigate that gave me so much trouble."

"From what you and Dresser told me she gave you very little trouble."

"True, but I don't think any captain without my experience and familiarity with the area would have done as well."

"Aren't you bragging a little?"

Matthew laughed. "Maybe, but I want to rid our primary trading area of that French pox first. Then I'll go after some other Frenchies."

"Now to the officers' changes again. Linthicum will be going ashore right away."

"What? I thought you liked him," said Eric.

"I do, and he's a fine seagoing lieutenant."

"So?"

"Seagoing is not the only thing he can do," explained Matthew. "He'll do a lot more for us by running the export-import business."

"And will we share in its profits?"

"Yes. I'm to be his partner."

Eric whistled. "That can be a lot of money. I can already see what the outgoing cargo meant to us. The merchants in town and from Baltimore are already lining up to see Dresser to buy the imported cargo and to make arrangements to get in on the next voyage."

"By the way. Where is he?" asked Matthew.

"In his new office downtown."

"But he just got home."

"His wife was alredy there."

"Ellen! You mean she got their office ready?"

"Elizabeth tells me she's a whirlwind in this business and probably would also be in any other business. Elizabeth wants to join her for a few months until the baby arrives."

"But pregnant women don't work in offices."

"You are behind the times. They are starting to do a lot of different things."

"And I suppose John Paul will take over from Elizabeth as draftsman?"

"Already has. If you'd come to work a litle earlier you'd catch up with what's going on."

"But she was here this morning."

"Feminine curiosity. She wanted to hear what you had to say before she left for her new job."

"You keep getting me off the main subject."

"Which is?"

"Officers."

"And?"

"Jarrell and MacClaren will go to sea with me on the first voyage of the *Mary* as a privateer. As I said, Jensen will leave to take over the next merchant ship, and Scotty MacIntosh or Jarrell will take over from me someday. For the next voyage I'll need a replacement for Linthicum."

"I'm going up to Jones Jebediah's tavern to have a little conversation with him."

"You mean you want him to come back to sea with you on the *Mary?*"

"Just that. Do you think the crew will object to a black officer?"

"Hell, no. It's common these days. Besides they still think of Jebediah as almost equal to you at sea."

Matthew grinned. "But not better."

"Right. But he was very good. Go on and see him."

Matthew walked up the street to the Jones Tavern. Jones Jebediah had taken the first name "Jones" in honor of his former commanding officer, Captain John Paul Jones, who had also taken the name "Jones" as an honorary last name. Jebediah junior was one of the elder Jebediah's sons, but he had never been given a first name. Jones Jebediah had named his tavern "The Jones" after John Paul Jones.

Matthew entered the impressive front door and paused just inside so his eyes could become accustomed to the lower light. There was no mistaking Jones Jebediah, even in the subdued light. His six-foot-four frame carried two hundred and twenty pounds of solid muscle. His face brightened at the sight of Matthew. He was glad to see his old captain.

Jebediah got down from his bar stool and ran over to Matthew. He clapped him in his huge arms. "Captain, where the hell have you been? Don't you like good grits? You know I serve the best meals in town."

"Oh, yes, but I've been away on a trip to the Caribbean, or I'd have been in here often. And please remember to call me by my first name. I'm no longer your captain."

"I will, and I wish I'd been with you. I heard about it, but it was too late to join you."

"I'd like to take you with me as a lieutenant as soon as I can convert the *Mary* to a privateer."

Jebediah scratched his chin. "That would fit in fine, but are you sure its legal?"

"I haven't heard that it isn't."

"Neither have I."

"You haven't been listening to your customers. They must have been talking about it."

Jebediah shrugged. "Well. I've got to admit that I haven't been in the place much lately."

"Women?"

"Oh, yes. Always them. They keep me busy."

"I've got a proposition for you. How about some prize money?"

Jebediah scratched his chin. "I've been losing money here, and I need some to tide me over until times get better. Also I'd like to get away from the local women for awhile."

"We'll square away the details as soon as I can get my young son to sea."

"Bruce?"

"Yes. He's going to be a midshipman on the new frigate, the *United States*."

"He'll be a fine one."

"Come by the shipyard when you're ready to join the ship."

Jebediah nodded. "All right, Matthew. Well, that didn't last long. Now I've got to call you 'captain' again, but I like it better anyway."

Chapter 15

The next morning Bruce Christopher finished his breakfast early. He needed a lot of food to keep his six feet and two hundred pounds full of calories. His dark hair was cut short, but even his ugly haircut failed to detract from his handsome features. If the girls thought he was handsome, he failed to acknowledge it. He was modest, though not shy, and the mothers of the community wished he would pay more attention to their daughters. "Too busy," he would say to his mother. "I'll get to them some day."

His father came down the stairs and looked at the big grandfather clock in the hall. "I see we have an hour before you go off to school."

"Yes, Father, and I had a feeling you wanted to talk to me this morning."

"I got a letter from Captain John Barry today. Do you know who he is?"

"Of course. He's to be the captain of the new frigate *United States.*"

"I have a feeling you already know everything I'm about to tell you."

Bruce grinned, his handsome face aglow. At 17 his muscles were beginning to show through his school shirt, and Matthew could see the coming need for a larger wardrobe. Bruce said, "A lot of it is common knowledge. I'm to report as a midshipman after the end of school next June."

"Well, stop dawdling and get to school. Since tomorrow is Saturday, we'll go downtown to my tailor and order your uniforms. At the rate you are eating and growing, they will have to be altered frequently."

The next morning Bruce and Matthew walked downtown to Matthew's tailor, where they ordered two sets of midshipmen's uniforms including dress items. A sword with its belt and a boat cloak completed the kit. Matthew explained to Bruce, "Of course you can get some oil skins and watch standing gear from the purser. Also a heavy weather jacket and boots."

Bruce looked at the growing pile on the counter. "How do I carry all these things?"

"We'll take it home in paper bags, fold it neatly and tightly, except for one uniform you'll wear, and stow it in a sea bag."

"Sea bag?"

"Yes. You'll find one in my closet. The name "Christopher" is already stencilled on it."

"I saw it up in the attic. I didn't know what it was when I saw it."

"Now you do. I brought it downstairs, and you'll see a lot of it from now on."

––––––––

The next afternoon when Bruce came home from school there was a letter for him from Captain John Barry. Bruce opened it eagerly as his mother looked over his shoulder.

Bruce smiled as he read it. "It tells me the ship will be commissioned 11 July, 1797. I'll be needed on board in the spring of 1798, and the remainder of the crew will be taken aboard soon after that."

"Then your father, after last Saturday's shopping trip, has you well outfitted and ready?" asked Martha.

"Oh, yes. He always does things well in advance, and this time is no exception."

"When will the ship be ready?"

"She'll go to sea in early July 1798."

"By the way, Mister Joshua Humphreys, the builder of your ship, has invited your father and me to attend the commissioning. Would you like to go?"

Bruce grinned widely. "Of course I would, there won't be any school on that day."

––––––––

On the 7th of July, Matthew handed Martha, Ellen, and Bruce into a rented carriage. Each brought only one bag,

"Because the space in the packet is limited," Matthew had told Ellen, who protested vehemently.

Matthew looked anxiously at his watch. "Can't keep the packet captain waiting," he replied.

Martha remarked, "He will try to leave on time, but Eric is on the landing with his hand on the brow and won't let it be taken in until we cross it."

Matthew grinned. "Just the same, get your petticoats in a hustle."

"Do we get the stateroom?" Ellen asked, remembering the previous trip to Philadelphia when she had slept in the room and later had met Dresser.

"You do. Bruce and I will have to sling hammocks in the main salon."

Bruce was hesitant, never having travelled in a packet before. "I guess I'll make it."

Matthew laughed. "Young man, for a future midshipman, this will be luxurious."

Ellen asked. "Father, why are we going to Philadelphia so early?"

"Ask your Mother. She wanted to have at least two days to shop."

Ellen brightened. "Good. I'll be able to spend some of the money I've earned."

"How is Dresser's business?"

"You ought to know. It's half yours."

"Just being polite. I happen to know it's doing very well, and you are part of the reason for its success. Dresser has given you credit for it."

"Dresser is very kind. I'd like to say you are the sole reason he's doing so well, but your part of the business has slowed while you were converting your ships, so he has turned to other shippers. He expects to do very well when you have the two new merchant ships."

The party arrived at the landing just in time, and Eric helped the group load their baggage before allowing the fuming captain to leave. The captain glared at Eric and spat in the direction of the horses. Eric glared right back, but no words or blows were exchanged.

"Damned old fool!" the captain muttered. "Him and his fancy horses."

"I heard you," Eric said. "Your ship isn't so fancy either. Your rigging needs attention and there's a lot of trash on your deck."

The captain ignored Eric and got the packet underway. On their previous trip, Martha and Ellen had retired immediately to the stateroom. This time they stayed on deck, watching the passing shore of the Chesapeake Bay as they sailed south and delighting in the flights of the sea birds following the packet.

"Fascinating," Ellen said. "The gulls are so graceful and beautiful."

Martha leaned lightly on the rail. "I can watch them for hours, but I think we ought to rest so we're ready to spend a lot of your father's money tomorrow morning."

Ellen said, "Mother, you forget I'll be spending my own money this time."

"You mean Dresser's?"

"No. I mean my own. I earned all of it."

Martha sighed. "Times certainly do change. I never earned a cent after I was married."

The next day, after the ladies had departed for the larger Philadelphia stores, Matthew informed Bruce of his appointment with Joshua Humphreys to be shown the *United States*. He invited Bruce to go with him.

Bruce asked, "Should I wear my uniform?"

Matthew laughed. "Oh, no. You won't be a midshipman for several months. The captain will order you to report about the first of June and will swear you in then. You should wear civilian clothes today. Let's go."

A rented carriage took them to the Humphreys' shipyard, and a man waiting for them at the gate led the carriage to

Humphreys' office.

Joshua Humphreys was waiting for the pair and greeted them warmly. Humphreys looked at Bruce appraisingly. "So this is our new midshipman. He's as big as you are, Matthew."

"Yes sir, I would like to present Bruce Christopher. I took the liberty of bringing him with me to see the ship."

"Of course. He is welcome. As a matter of fact, Captain Barry is aboard and said he would like to meet you both. Let's go to the fitting out dock."

The ship was riding smoothly in a southerly wind, tugging gently at her mooring lines. To Matthew's trained eye she seemed to be beautifully designed, but he could not tell how well she had been built. He knew of Humphreys' reputation as a designer and builder, but he had heard rumors of labor trouble and shortage of funds. Congress had grown increasingly stingy as the true costs of their authorized programs became apparent. Nevertheless, he was sure that any shortcomings in the beautiful ship would be corrected soon. He determined not to embarrass Humphreys by posing penetrating questions. This was a social visit.

Humphreys led Matthew and Bruce up the steep brow towering almost three stories over the ground. The ship was not yet commissioned and therefore no colors were flying.

The tour started forward and below, since the topside was not yet finished, and the workmen were preparing it for the upcoming ceremony. Humphreys explained the new methods of construction as they came to them. Matthew looked at the new diagonal system Humphreys had told him about on his previous visit. The diagonals were fixed between the futtocks. Humphreys explained, "This will strengthen the ship's side by thirty percent."

As they proceeded aft along the lower deck, Humphreys pointed to a small dark enclosure to port. "This is the midshipmens' wardroom and quarters. It will be more comfortable when it is completely finished."

Bruce looked at it and shook his head doubtfully.

Matthew tried to hurry them past the area.

"What's the next space?" he asked.

Humphreys said, "Oh, this is the officers' wardroom. It's a bit small, but it will do."

Bruce noted that the small staterooms resembled horses' stalls and were little bigger. They were almost as bad as the midshipmen's quarters. Bruce wondered why so little space was allocated to them while the ship seemed to be so spacious otherwise.

The answer came to him as they walked farther aft. The captain's quarters occupied about half of the space for berthing on the berth deck. A removable bulkhead shut off well over 30 feet of the after part of the deck from one side to the other. Some of this space was occupied by the carriages of twenty-four pounders, but most of it was devoted to the captain's comfort.

Matthew shook his head again but said nothing.

Humphreys, noting Matthew's reaction, but mistaking it for approval, sought confirmation. "Not bad, eh?" he asked.

Matthew could hold in his disapproval no longer. "Seems to me to be overly-spacious," he said. "Just as the midshipman's and officer's space is very small."

Humphreys seemed to miss the point. "Well, we always want to make our captains comfortable. After all, they carry a heavy responsibility."

Matthew looked at the copper stove designed to heat this space and the large mahogany table with its ten windsor chairs. Other chairs lined the bulkhead between the guns. "He certainly will be comfortable," he said without enthusiasm.

As they passed quickly aft, Joshua said, "The captain's personal quarters occupy the rest of the berth deck. Captain Barry is in and is expecting us. I'll knock."

Humphreys knocked firmly on the heavy door and stood back. Since the ship was not yet commissioned, there was no Marine complement yet aboard and there was no sentry posted before Barry's door.

The captain opened the door himself and he stepped back. "Ah, Humphreys, I've been expecting you and your guests. Please come in." Barry was a large man, going to fat. His head was large and square, topped by a shock of graying hair. His features were regular and strong, dominated by piercing blue eyes. There was no doubt that this man was the captain of the ship.

The interior had been luxuriously furnished, and Bruce could see six curtained windows aft and open doors on the sides, revealing two sizeable staterooms furnished with large beds, water closets, and large bathtubs.

Humphreys introduced Matthew and Bruce to the Captain, and Barry invited them to sit down. "Sorry," he said, "I do not have a steward yet, so I can't offer you any refreshment. However, there will be refreshments topside after the forthcoming ceremony. I understand there will be places reserved for you and your ladies."

Matthew nodded. "Yes, sir, thank you. And my family is eagerly looking forward to attending. It should be an impressive ceremony."

Barry looked carefully at Bruce. "Young man, I understand you will be 18 and a college graduate when you report to me. How much experience have you had at sea?"

"My father taught me seamanship and navigation, and I have been at sea for three summers as a seaman. I believe I am qualified to perform all the duties of a midshipman."

Barry slapped his knee and laughed. "You certainly are one of the best qualified midshipmen I'll have and probably the oldest. Most of them will be political appointees." Barry shuddered. "I have to take that into account and look to young men like you to perform the real work."

Bruce remained silent, but Captain Barry continued, "Promotion is somewhat the same. Commissions for lieutenants are usually granted by members of the Congresses' Marine Committee to personal favorites. That means you will never see a commission in normal conditions. But do not despair. I have authority to award lieutenant's commissions at sea under combat or urgent weather conditions to those I consider deserving. I'll be watching you, and I guarantee I'll make awards for all those who perform outstandingly."

Humphreys stirred, realizing they were keeping the captain too long from his duties, and said, "Well, Captain, thank you for your time. They will see you next at the ceremony."

"Ah, of course Humphreys. Could you possibly stay a few minutes and remind me of the arrangements for the event?"

"Certainly, but if you'll permit me, I'd like to see my guests out first."

Matthew interrupted him. "Thank you, Joshua, but we can find our way off the ship. Thank you for a wonderful day, and I will see you on the 11th."

———•———

Back at the hotel Bruce sat before a lemonade, uncharacteristically glum. "What's the matter, son?" Matthew asked.

Bruce shook his head. "I liked the ship and its captain, but not the midshipmen's and officer's quarters. They looked like a prison."

Matthew nodded. "I told you you wouldn't like going to sea."

Bruce grinned wryly and shook his head. "I know there will be many hardships, bad weather, battle, poor food, long hours. But when I saw what midshipmen and even officers must endure compared to the spacious palace the captain lives in, my stomach turned."

Matthew cleared his throat. "You can get used to anything, and I'll guarantee that you won't spend much time in your quarters."

———•———

The eleventh, the day set for the commissioning, was beautiful but hot. Matthew rented a carriage and suggested that Martha and Ellen carry parasols. The morning ceremony would still be hot in early July.

The Christopher party pulled up to the bottom of the brow. They got out and looked up at the magnificent ship towering above them. The brow was decorated with red, white, and blue bunting, and signal flags flew from wherever they could be placed.

Martha remarked, "But there aren't any colors flying."

Matthew laughed. "There will be when the captain declares the ship commissioned."

The party made its way up the brow where they were greeted by members of Joshua's staff, escorted to the quarterdeck aft, and seated. A group of Joshua's staff and workmen filled one side of the quarterdeck, and a small contingent of officers and enlisted men from Captain Barry's crew filled the other side. Matthew poked Bruce to get his attention. "See. The bottoms of the staffs and the gaff where the colors, the union jack, and the commission pennant will be flown, are manned by members of the crew, who will raise the appropriate flags at the moment the captain declares the ship is commissioned."

Bruce nodded. "I understand they will hoist the appropriate flags."

Matthew said, "Not exactly raise them. You'll see."

Promptly at 10 a.m. Captain Barry appeared on deck, escorted by Joshua Humphreys. Both went to a lectern placed on the quarterdeck.

Humphreys introduced a waiting clergyman who offered a short prayer. Humphreys then introduced Captain Barry, who rose and bowed.

The Captain strode to the lectern, placed a set of notes on it, and stood back. He looked around at the ship and the assembly before clearing his throat dramatically. He began in a deep voice, "Ladies and gentlemen, officers and men of the crew, and those of you who built this fine vessel, well done. I commend the Congress and taxpayers who made this ship possible. I ask the blessings of the Lord on her, and may she serve her country well. Now I will read my orders from the Marine Committee of the Congress and the

Secretary of the Navy."

When he had read his orders, he raised his voice even further and ordered, "I hereby place this vessel in commission in the United States Navy! Break the flags! Members of the crew previously detailed, set the watch!"

The men standing by the flag staffs at the bow and stern and the halliards at the bottom of the main mast pulled firmly on the bottom halliards. Simultaneously, small strings placed around the neatly folded flags broke and released the flags into the breeze.

Martha gasped. Even Bruce was surprised. Martha exclaimed, "That was beautiful! You didn't tell me it was going to that way."

Matthew grinned. "I thought it would be more impressive as a surprise. This is probably the only commissioning ceremony you will ever see."

It was a moving occasion, but Matthew's thoughts were already on the *Mary* as they filed forward to the waiting refreshments. This was Bruce's party, but Matthew wanted to get back to Annapolis as soon as possible to go to sea.

Chapter 16

That evening the family enjoyed the dining room in their Philadelphia hotel. Bruce looked around at the room's decorations. "This beats the Middletown Tavern or Jebediah's Tavern, although he's pretty good with tassels."

Martha looked around and said loyally, "It's pretty, but not that good. We'll want to see how the food is."

Ellen bristled. "Oh, Mother, you know it's beautiful. You aren't a big city girl."

Matthew interrupted, "Let up on the decorations and study the menu. I'm getting quite hungry, and I don't care how the room looks."

They settled on steak, but Ellen finally changed her mind. "I can eat steak at home. I want to try a French dish."

Matthew rolled his eyes. "Choose any one, but get on with it. I'm starving, and I still want steak."

Ellen giggled. "My French lacks something. That's why I want to go back to school when I get established in business."

"I'd say you are established now. And if you don't choose soon, I'll pick something on the menu for you. My French is not very good either."

When the dinner arrived, and Matthew inspected everyone's dish. "Looks good," he pronounced.

He cut his steak carefully. "Beats any beef this side of Pittsburgh!"

Bruce grinned. "Jones Tavern has better beef."

When Matthew got the bill for dinner, his eyebrows shot up and he whistled. "These city types have found a way to keep profits up. They just continue raising the prices. This bill would feed a small ship."

Ellen looked at the bill and laughed. "The cheapest item on your bill is my French dish."

The next morning, after the ladies had settled in the packet's stateroom, Matthew took Bruce forward, and both of them leaned on the rail as the little ship left Philadelphia. The upperworks of the *United States* were visible as they towered over Humphreys' shipyard. Matthew pointed her out. "She's a beautiful ship."

Bruce hesitated, then he said in a low voice, "Beautiful outside, but little better than a chicken coop inside, and a small one at that."

Matthew could sense his feeling, and he said, "Son, you are unhappy. Do you want to call off all this? There's still enough time."

Bruce laughed and straightened up. "No, Dad. I'm not a quitter. I know this will be tough and tiresome, but I can take it if the other midshipmen can."

"But you are expecting to get a reasonable reward some day if you last out the course?"

"I wouldn't call it a reward. Just a chance to fight fairly for promotions and a command some day."

"You heard what Joshua Humphreys and Captain Barry said. Promotions can be very slow and they almost always go to the wrong man," Matthew said.

"Of course. That's the way the country has become. In the Royal Navy, advancement comes from aristocratic position established by birth. In our navy, it's a little different, but just as bad. Our navy has become a cesspool of political influence. We are made officers because our fathers know a Congressmen and usually buy their favors."

"You mean with money?"

"Sometimes. I suspect they trade favors or influence just as much."

Matthew said, "And I don't have influence?"

"I don't think so, or if you had, I don't think you'd use it. You are too honest."

"Well, you're right" confirmed Matthew. "And I do have money. Maybe not enough, but I wouldn't be a party to buying a Congressman. I realize this means I'm leaving you out in the cold all by yourself."

Bruce smiled, "Dad, I wouldn't have it any other way. I'll make it on my own or not at all."

"You know you can always have a position in one of our shipyards or on one of our ships. After have been a midshipman, I can make you a lieutenant without offending anybody else."

"Oh, let it ride for awhile. I'm confident I can make it on my own."

"And you think you can beat the system?"

"You heard Captain Barry admit that when it came to promotion at sea he had to give priority to those who performed best. His life, his career, and the success of his ship depend on putting the best officers in positions of authority."

"And you think this will happen?" asked Matthew.

"It has to. Captain Barry said it would, and I expect to be the best midshipman he has when it comes time to appoint one to lieutenant."

"Well, son, I agree with you and I am very proud of you. You will go far."

They talked late into the night, discussing Matthew's experience and his feelings for the sea. The navigational lights along the river channel rolled by, and the stars remained bright.

About midnight Matthew yawned. "You young boys can take these late hours better than I can. I'm going to turn in."

Bruce laughed. "I was told you stayed up several nights in a row when you were in command of the *Mary.*"

Matthew grinned in the dark. "So will you when you are in command. There is something about the responsibility that enables you to keep going without sleep for a long time. Good night."

Chapter 17

Matthew paced the decks of the packet as it glided into a landing on the Annapolis waterfront. He left Eric to take the ladies, Bruce, and the baggage home and trotted up the street to the shipyard office.

"What ails him?" Eric asked Martha as he watched Matthew's retreating form.

Martha shrugged. "Oh, you know what it is. He can hardly wait to get the *Mary* ready to go to sea. There was gossip all over Philadelphia about what the French are doing, and it roused him up."

"Anything about what the Congress is doing regarding privateer laws?"

Martha shook her head. "You'll have to ask Matthew. I don't understand these complicated matters."

Eric sighed as he hauled himself into the driver's seat and picked up the reins. He looked back at Martha. "If Congress does the right thing in a timely manner, Matthew can come home rich and free. If they stall, as they have been, he might go to France in chains."

Ellen frowned. "What does that mean?"

Martha shrugged. "These international politics are too much for me. I only care whether or not Matthew comes home. That's what counts."

Eric whipped the horses and they went flying up the street. Martha and Ellen had trouble keeping their hats on and their skirts down. Martha said, "Watch out, Eric. These old men on the sidewalk are getting a free show."

Eric laughed. "All right, I'll pull them in. We are only a block away. Besides you two are the best show in town, and they love it."

Eric quickly unloaded his passengers and their baggage and left Bruce in charge of getting them in the house. He turned his horses, tipped his hat to the ladies, jammed it on his head, and whipped the horses. In a few minutes he was back at the shipyard office, making one of his famous landings in front of the hitching rack. He threw the reins over the rack, and without bothering to tie them, shouted at the clerk nearest the door, "Jerry, please feed my horses and tie them up. Now where the hell is Matthew?"

Jerry, on his way out, pointed towards Matthew. "At the drafting table. Where else?"

Eric clomped over to his son. "Matthew, why the hell did you leave me behind? I want to know what happened in Philadelphia to cause you to run up the street when you got back."

Matthew sighed. "Nothing exactly. There were rumors all over Philadelphia that the French are intensifying their sea war against us."

"Hell, I can guess that, but what is the Congress doing these days?"

"Pussyfooting as usual. I think they'll pass laws permitting us to privateer. Maybe they'll even abrogate our treaties with France if the situation gets bad enough."

"But when?" Eric asked.

"My guess is July."

"What? Are you going to wait until July to send our new merchant ship to Havana and the *Mary* to sea?"

Matthew nodded. "Yes. It will be a risk, but I hope I'll be able to escort it. Now what's holding up progress on the *Mary*? I thought we'd be ready soon."

"The trouble is the foundry in Philapelphia."

"I thought they'd make the best guns for us. They would be capable of using a larger powder charge and the guns would therefore have a longer range than any in the world of the same size."

"Yes," Eric said, "We have the world's best iron ore recently discovered out in the middle west. Our coal produces fine coke. Our foundry workers learned their trade in Europe. And then something went wrong."

"Well?"

Eric shrugged. "They keep giving us excuses. Maybe you should take a trip up there."

"I will. Now what else do we have to talk about?"

"Well, your son John Paul is turning into a very inventive ship designer. He has devised a way to set rings down in the deck to secure the falls the gunners use to haul back the guns. As you know, presently this rigging hinders the gunners on the guns behind them."

"Yes. That has always been a drawback of using the narrow hulls required with schooner rigs. It is a price we pay for added speed."

"Well, John Paul's scheme permits the falls to be disconnected from the ring when not needed, and the ring falls into the deck out of the way. The gun crews on the other side can work right over the top of it," said Eric.

"Sounds good. What else?" Matthew asked.

"He has improved the rigging so that a man, or maybe two, can be cut from each watch. He has also worked with the gunner to save 12 men in the gun crews."

"Good. That permits me to form another prize group from the same number of crewmen."

Eric looked at his watch. "Well, that's enough of this small stuff. You'd better get packed and ready for the packet to Philadelphia."

———————

Two days later, Matthew sat in a hired carriage in Pittsburgh, drumming impatiently on the seat's arm as he urged the driver to speed up. At the foundry office, Matthew leaped out of the carriage and strode rapidly up to the door. Inside he asked to see the owner. A solidly built Dutchman received him. "Yes, what can I do for you?"

"My name is Matthew Christopher. You've been working on an order for 28 guns for my two ships. They are a month overdue, and I need them badly. What's the trouble?"

The Dutchman shrugged. "You know we make the best guns in the world?"

"Yes, but where are they?"

"Well, I say they are still in the Minnesota mines."

"And what causes that?"

"The mine is still on strike. Lucky for us we have plenty of coke but no iron ore."

"And now what?"

"No iron ore, no guns."

"How long do you think the strike will last?" "Perhaps a month."

———

Matthew rode back to the packet landing silently cursing all the way. Two days later, after the trip south, he was back in his office, still glowering.

Eric grinned. "See, you didn't do any better than I did by mail."

"I can't just wait. I'll get my crew together and train them on the stern chaser guns."

"Good. That should work off some of your frustration."

———

The delay permitted Matthew to complete his crew and load his ship.

Exactly one month later, on the first of June, the guns arrived by lighter and were hastily loaded aboard. The new merchant ship, now captained by Jensen, completed loading on the fifth of June, and both ships promptly departed. Matthew had reviewed with Jensen the tactics he had used to enter Havana and Matanzas Harbors.

Matthew explained to Jensen, "You won't need to use them unless I am delayed. I intend to arrive a day ahead of you and take the French privateer as my first prize. I'll cruise off the coast until you are ready, and then we'll all come home together."

Chapter 18

Matthew began test firing his new guns almost immediately after they lost sight of the Chesapeake Bay. When Matthew and his gunner, Velasquez were satisfied that the individual guns showed no signs of casting flaws or errors and that the handling tackle was installed satisfactorily, Matthew began the test firing of each gun, starting with a half powder load. Then he increased the powder load by 25 percent to 20 percent overload. He had no ready method of gauging the range he was getting, but Velasquez guessed it was 25 percent over any range of that weight of gun he had ever seen fired. As they fired, the guns recoiled more than usual because of the extra powder charge, but there were no signs of metal failure.

The testing of all guns took a full day, and at the end of it Matthew declared himself completely satisfied. Velasquez was ecstatic, declaring that he had never seen such range before. On the next day, both ships sailed out into the Atlantic and set course for Havana.

Matthew kept his crew at loading and firing exercises until he was satisfied that each sailor was carrying out his individual task while cooperating smoothly, so that each man from powder boy to gun captain, knew his job and the safety precautions.

On the fourth day Matthew signalled to Jensen that he was proceeding ahead at best speed and expected to arrive off Havana Harbor in two days.

Matthew conducted a final run-through at full speed with his gun crews, and they practiced tacking and maneuvering the ship while simulating firing.

On the night before he expected to arrive off Havana, Matthew conducted a final briefing of his officers. MacClaren was an old hand and Jarrell and Velasquez were experienced and used to his methods. Jones Jebediah had the advantage of having served with Matthew in battle many times. Matthew had only to brief him on the geography of Havana and he spent several hours going over what he anticipated.

When he was satisfied, he directed all hands to turn in early and to be on stations two hours before dawn.

The next morning, MacClaren reported that the crew had been fed breakfast and were at quarters. Matthew nodded to him. "This will be a grand day for us. That bastard caused me a lot of apprehension, although he never bloodied us. Still, I want him to pay."

Just at dawn, with the entrance to Havana Harbor directly ahead, the lookout shouted, "Sail ho! Dead ahead!"

Matthew shouted aloft, "Can you make her out?"

The lookout answered, "Too dark yet, sir."

Matthew could wait no longer. He grabbed a long glass, shoved it down his belt, narrowly missing his testicles, and climbed rapidly up the ratlines. Soon he could see the outline of the sails the lookout had reported. With his long glass he could tell it was a three-masted frigate. As the light increased, he thought it was the French frigate, and in a few more minutes he was sure.

He slid down the ratlines quickly, giving more care to storing his long glass this time.

"Jesus!" he thought, "Martha says she has no more need for me after our five children, but she might change her mind. I've got to be more careful."

When he reached the deck he yelled, "We're coming up on her from astern. Hoist all sail and check your guns. She's idling along probably either at breakfast or asleep. They never think of looking astern. Jarrell, stay on your present course."

"Aye, aye, sir," Jarrell answered.

Matthew said, "Pass the word for both battery officers to

lay aft."

Velasquez now commanded the port battery and Jebediah had taken over the starboard battery. When they were both on the quarterdeck, Matthew said, "If they see us suddenly and react promptly we'll open up with the bow chasers. If we can get close enough to get in range before either of us fires, I plan to change course to starboard to clear the port battery. After we fire that battery, I'll change course to port to clear the other battery. If we hit, and we will, I think there is a good chance that we'll clear her quarterdeck and will damage her steering system. Then we'll have her at our mercy."

The battery officers ran forward up the deck to their expectant men and briefed their gun captains. The light gradually increased as the *Mary,* all sails drawing, drew rapidly up behind the unsuspecting frigate.

Matthew paced the quarterdeck anxiously, stopping frequently to glare at the French ship through his long glass. When he was sure they were in range, even for the new guns, he shouted, "Alter course to starboard! Port battery commence firing when you bear!"

The next few seconds were anxious ones for the crew, many of whom had not seen action, but for Matthew they were precious. He was sure he was going to surprise the Frenchman, and then it would be so easy!

On the *Mary's* decks, the crew was laughing and shouting, watching the French sailors.

Velasquez could stand it no longer. "Silence!" he roared. "Pay attention to your duties and let those clowns over there make the noise!"

Then Velasquez noticed a powder boy standing beside him. The lad was carrying four powder bags in an apron-like contraption designed to allow the carrying of four powder bags from the magazines to the guns. Velasquez raised his voice again. "Lad, don't just stand there! This is not a sporting event! Take the powder to the guns. They are waiting for it!"

But the boy seemed to be paralyzed by the loudness of Velaquez's voice. Velasquez lost his patience and raised his hand to backhand the boy, who cringed, expecting the blow.

"Damn!" Velsquez said, "I'm sorry. I didn't think. If I'd hit you, you might have dropped a powder bag. If it broke open, there would have been powder all over the deck, and pieces of burning wadding might have set it off. I'm sorry. Now go about your business and be very careful. Our lives are in your hands."

Matthew heard the last part of the dialogue and tried to change the tone of the exchange. "You were right," he said to his gunner, "And I think he has learned his lesson."

The Matthew turned his attention to the French ship, still sailing serenely ahead. The *Mary* swung rapidly, and in seconds the guns boomed out. Matthew climbed far enough up the ratlines to see over the cloud of smoke. He counted the seconds of the expected time of flight. Then some of the balls ripped through the large lower course sails, and he could see others landing on the quarterdeck. Splinters of decking and rails flew up. One large piece of railing turned over and over as it sailed into the sea. "The bastards," he thought. "Just thieves, highwaymen, pirates!" He took a deep breath and tried to control his rage, but it was useless.

Jarrell heard him muttering. "Captain, what's the trouble?"

"I keep thinking how many of our ships the French have taken, and how many of our men are in those filthy French prisons."

"Yes, I know. Someday we'll sweep the seas and push them back into their pox-ridden ports."

"One ship at a time. This will be a small revenge for our country, but it will help," said Matthew.

Then it was time. "Come left!" he shouted. "Starboard battery fire when you bear!"

The second course change required more time than the first and Matthew grew impatient watching the French crew scurry about the decks. Then the *Mary* came about more rapidly as the helmsman spun the wheel with all his might.

The next broadside detonated almost as one explosion. The thunderous roll made his ears sing. Matthew let out his breath. "Let me know when you're ready for the next broadside!"

He looked at the ship ahead, now so close he did not need the long glass. The last salvo landed, and he could see easily that the quarterdeck was a shambles. Jarrell said, "She's lost steering, and I think all those on the quarterdeck are dead. The bodies are in piles."

Some of the Frenchmen were looking aft at the *Mary* and shaking their fists. Matthew laughed exultantly. "Those apes should be going to their guns instead of swearing at us. Typical Frenchmen. Don't fight. Just yell. Well, while they're squawking we'll put a lot of shot into her."

Jarrell coughed from the gun smoke, and when he cleared his eyes and throat, he looked at the French ship. Matthew's eyes cleared first, and he lost no time giving the next order.

"Well, we'll still get another salvo off unless she strikes her colors."

Just as Matthew opened his mouth to give the order, the quartermaster shouted, "Sir, she has struck her colors!"

Matthew pounded his fist on the rail. "It's over," he said, "And they didn't even fire at us! Not even a stern chaser!"

The frigate's sails fluttered down, and she began to wallow in the medium seas. As they ran alongside, Matthew shouted, "Jarrell, down sails. Make a boat ready for our prize crew!"

Jebediah came running aft, carrying a small bag and a sword. "Well, Captain, here I am. You told me I'd command the first prize."

Matthew grinned. "Your first command and not your last. I want to send you out in command of one of our ships soon. You'll be just the man."

Jebediah smiled broadly. "I'm ready, but I may be too old."

"When you get over there, let me know if you need any help in repairing her steering system. Our new merchant ship will be arriving tomorrow, and we'll be lying off Havana Harbor for about four days. Then we'll move to Matanzas for a short period of about four days. That should give you plenty of time for repairs."

Jebediah saluted, "Aye, aye, Captain."

"One more thing. I'm sending over the other boat loaded with armed men and our surgeon. I don't know what you'll find over there. You can use some of the armed men to round up, disarm, and lock up the able bodied men. The surgeon will help with the wounded."

"I'll send them back, Captain, as soon as I've made repairs and I feel safe."

"I want you to continue feeling safe. I am sending with you three lanterns, red, white, and blue. Also three pennants of the same colors for daytime use. Here's a code to use. It tells you to show from a yard arm two colors of lanterns or pennants. The code changes every four hours. If at any time the code isn't being followed correctly, I'll know something is wrong and I'll be over with a boarding party in minutes. One other thing. I'm sending an American flag with you. Keep the American flag up when we're alone. If a French ship shows up soon, follow my movements in hoisting a French flag. That way we may lure the relieving French ship into firing range or even close aboard. They will recognize the shape of your ship or the cut of your sails. When the French ship arrives, let me fight her, and you pull out of range."

"Sounds like it will be an eventful Saturday night on the Havana waterfront."

Matthew watched the boats being rowed to the French frigate and felt very satified. Now he would hopefully add a couple of prizes on the way back and maybe the relief French frigate if she were on the way south. He shook his head and said to Jarrell, "It would be nice to know when the French frigate's relief will arrive."

Jarrell laughed, "Why don't you tell Jebediah to ask the French. They should know, if anyone over there is still alive. I am sure he can find out."

Chapter 19

Early the next morning the company merchant ship arrived. Captain Jensen waved at Matthew, who pointed at the French frigate prize following the *Mary*.

Jensen grinned and waved again. Matthew pointed at the entrance to Havana Harbor and watched as Jensen steered his ship for it.

Matthew shouted at Jarrell who was across the quarterdeck watching their prize. "Jarrell, lower a boat to take me over to ask Jebediah if he has found out anything about the approximate arrival date of the French relief ship."

Matthew climbed up the sea ladder of the frigate nimbly and was met by Jones Jebediah at the top. Jebediah was wearing his sword and two pistols in his belt.

Matthew said, "Captain, you look like business. Is everything safe?"

"Very. I'll send the extra armed men, the surgeon, and the carpenter back. Fortunately the French surgeon survived, and he can handle all the wounded by himself. We will bury the dead at noon today."

"Were there many casualties?"

"About half the crew was killed, and all but one officer who was asleep below. The surgeon has sewn all the dead in canvas with a ball at their feet. The custom in the French Navy seems to be the same as ours and the British."

"How are the repairs going?"

"Just about finished. I was able to steer her with a jury rig and am about to shift to a permanent repair job. I've used some of the French crew to break out spare sails, rigging, and cordage. The masts are essentially undamaged, and I'll be able to make ten knots soon, if the ship ever went that fast before."

Matthew looked up at the rigging carefully. "I can't see the shape of the sails, of course, but from the rigging and the shape of the hull above water, I'll guess at eight knots, maybe more."

"How is the crew?" Matthew asked.

"Fairly subdued. They know you will be close by, and they believe you have some magical powers. I've let them continue to think that." Jebediah grinned. "Of course I believe that too."

"I will be able to let more prisoners out as soon as I see how they are taking their defeat. I questioned the surviving officer and examined the Captain's papers. In them was a letter in which the French officer says the relief ship will arrive this week."

Matthew said. "Give the papers to me. I'll have Velasquez check them. His French is pretty good."

"I would have sent them over sooner, but I just found them a few moments ago."

Matthew laughed. "Just right, good work. We'll be ready. I want to use your ship as bait. When they come in sight, raise your French flag and look as much as you can as if you are still operating. I will do what I can to look like your prize. When he gets close enough, send him a signal for the captain to report aboard."

Jebediah grinned. "I'll have the French officer on the quarterdeck with a pistol at his back and a couple of my men dressed in French officer's uniforms. If the arriving captain balks I'll twitch the pistol in his back and have my French officer talk him aboard."

"Good. As soon as I see him aboard I'll open my gun ports and demand that the senior officer still aboard surrender."

"Should work, but I can't believe you can take two prizes without losing a man," marveled Jebediah.

"I haven't done it yet, but our plan is bold enough to work. Now I'm going back to my ship. If all is clear tomorrow, I'm going into Havana Harbor to call on my friend Juan Castro. As soon as I get back, move into the harbor and anchor as close as you can to Castro's pier. During the night transfer anything to Castro's men that is loose and that you won't need on the voyage back to Annapolis. If the French ship shows up, stop and come on out."

"But why, Captain?"

"Politics. You'll find out when we get home."

———•———

The horizon was clear the following morning, so Matthew moved the *Mary* into Havana Harbor and anchored close to Castro's pier. He was rowed ashore in a boat and walked to the door of Castro's office. Castro saw him coming, stepped out of his office, took out his cigar, and smiled. "Ah, mi amigo Captain Christopher. I am glad to see you."

"I am glad to be here, Señor Castro. How is business?"

"It wasn't so good for the past six months when your ships didn't show up. Now that one of your merchant ships is here, can I expect more frequent visits?"

"Yes. And safer ones. I captured the French frigate that was annoying all the ships trying to enter Havana Harbor. She won't bother either of us again, or anybody else, and I hope to take over the one that is supposed to come here this week to relieve her."

"Excellent, my friend. We will make lots of money now."

"Yes. I will soon have two merchant ships on regular runs about every month. The French will not be able to bother them. They will both be fast sailing ships they can't catch. I will guarantee to take any French ship that tries to patrol off the harbors of Cuba."

"Can you join us for dinner tonight? My wife enjoyed your last visit."

"I'm afraid not. I want to be back off the harbor entrance in case the next French frigate shows up. If I capture her I'll bring her in to unload her. She should be well supplied at the beginning of her voyage. In the meantime I'll send the ex-French frigate *Marie* in to unload. You can sell anything that isn't nailed down."

Castro chuckled. "You are one mean merchant. Why are

you doing this? You might make more from these types of supplies in your country."

"The Congress, my friend. They are meaner than I am, and they won't let me."

"I hear they may pass a law soon allowing privateers to keep all they capture, ships and cargo both. Now and then small ships cross the Florida Straits with news they pick up in the bars of Southern Florida."

"Of course I don't get any news at sea. I just know they are slow. If they haven't passed any new laws when I get back, I'll unload the prize cargo secretly and sell it."

"And the ships? Won't you have to turn the ships themselves over to your government?"

"Of course, but I won't."

"How can you get around the law?"

"I'll take the unloaded ships out in the bay and sink them."

Castro laughed. "You are a tough guy, as they say in your country."

Matthew soon returned to the entrance and sent Jebediah with the *Marie* in to the Castro pier. The *Marie* was quickly unloaded, and four days later the Martha finished unloading and was moved down the coast to Matanzas to take on a return cargo. Matthew continued to patrol off the Havana Harbor entrance, practicing communication with a quartermaster he had sent over to the *Marie*.

Two days later, the lookouts sighted a sail to the north and Matthew made all preparations in case it might be the expected French ship. He exchanged stations with the *Marie*, following astern of her. All extra hands were directed to go below or crouch behind the bulwarks. A few men were heavily bandaged, and Matthew put on a large white arm sling. He paced the quarterdeck, hoping that the ship was the one they were expecting.

Soon it became apparent that it was a three-masted frigate, and in a few minutes the lookouts could make out the French ensign. There was no doubt it was the expected guest.

The French frigate sailed on, obviously recognizing the ship she was to relieve. Her gun ports were still secured, and her crew was lounging about the decks. As arranged, Jebediah brought the *Marie* into the wind and Matthew kept his ship upwind. Instead of lowering his sails completely as Jebediah had done, Matthew kept men at the halliards ready to raise them quickly. The gun crews were crouched below the bulwarks ready to open the gun ports and run the guns out quickly.

The approaching French ship was not taking any precautions that Matthew could see. When she was abeam of Matthew's prize, she came into the wind to parallel her sister ship. Jebediah, with the help of his captive French officer, signalled to the commanding officer of the arriving French ship to come aboard immediately. At first there was some disagreement on the quarterdeck of the second French ship, but Jebediah prodded the captive French officer, providing a stream of indignant French. He told the other French captain to hurry and reminded him that his captain was senior. This action appeared to resolve the argument, and soon the French captain was rowed over to Jebediah's command. As soon as the captain was aboard, Jebediah directed the boat to pull away and hoisted his sails. As soon as he saw this, Matthew ordered his crew to open the gun ports and man their guns. Using his school French, he ordered through his speaking trumpet, "Surrender or I will sink you and order your captain killed."

The senior officer on the quarterdeck appeared to be startled and looked at the guns pointed at him. Jarrell said, "The little frog with the sword and all the gold must be the second senior officer and appears to want to surrender."

Matthew laughed. "But the others are bigger, and I am afraid they will out-argue him."

They did, and the men began to scurry to their guns.

Matthew shook his head. "Enough! Commence firing!"

Without hesitation, the broadside was fired and the grape

Matthew had had loaded swept the Frenchman's decks only yards away. When the smoke cleared, Matthew could see most of the crew down on the French ship and a few lucky souls holding up their hands. "Cease firing!" he shouted.

The only French officer still standing could be seen pointing at the colors, and a quartermaster crawled over and hauled down the colors.

Matthew yelled, "Away the prize crew! Lieutenant Jarrell, you will be in command. After you feel you are in control, lock up the crew and sail her into Havana Harbor. Unload all equipment that can be moved and all supplies except what you need to sail her back home."

Jarrell rubbed his chin. "I understand your orders and am prepared to carry them out, but what the hell for?"

Matthew grinned. "Just do it. I'll tell you why later."

The next morning Matthew moved his ship into Havana Harbor and watched the second French frigate being unloaded. He went ashore and visited Castro's office. "Amigo, you did it again!" said a smiling Castro.

Matthew laughed. "Here's the inventory of all of the stores and equipment the French captain said he was carrying. Can you handle this?"

Castro looked at the inventory and shrugged. "Certainly. All of it. We are unloading it now with the help of your capable Captain Jarrell. My operatives in Washington and Florida tell me you can't declare this as prize cargo yet. The ships of course aren't declarable either. They also tell me that your Congress will pass a law soon."

"That's my guess, but if I guess incorrectly and bring them back too soon, then I get nothing. Obviously you will take it all at discount except the ships."

Castro shrugged. "Not much discount. After all, you and I are almost partners, and I know you will bring me much business in the future. I treat you right. By the way, why do you stay in your country with its terrible Congress? Come down here and I will make you rich."

"Someone has to correct its errors. When we're ready I'll be taking these prizes home to turn them over to a prize court."

Castro chuckled. "But a little lighter than when you took them. Are you really going to turn them over?"

"It will depend on how I feel when I get home and have a chance to talk to my father and our company lawyer."

"And then what will you do?" asked Castro.

"As I told my officers, I may unload what is left, and then take the ships out in the bay and sink them."

Chapter 20

Two days later, when the company merchant ship had returned from Matanzas, Mathew called Jebediah and Jarrell over to the *Mary* for a conference.

When they had assembled, he strode up and down in the small cabin and began. "We're leaving for Annapolis right away. As we sail north I hope to take another prize or two. Jebediah will sail ten miles to my starboard, and Jarrell will take position ten miles to my port. Our merchant ship will take positon astern of me. This way we will sweep a 30 mile swath of ocean, hoping to capture someone in our net."

———

On the second day they did just that. The *Mary* lookouts yelled down, "Sail ho! Dead ahead!"

The sail grew larger slowly, and the lookouts added, "She is headed north, but we are overtaking her!"

Matthew nodded. "Make all sail. We should overtake her by dark."

They did. The sail proved to belong to a medium-sized merchant ship flying a French flag. She offered no resistance, and her crew consisted of mostly blacks from Haiti. Matthew ordered Velasquez to take over the prize.

———

As they made their way north sailing at least a hundred miles off the coast to avoid the weather off Cape Hatteras, Matthew hoped to take another prize. Unfortunately nothing showed up by the time the little flotilla arrived at the entrance to the Chesapeake Bay, so Matthew reluctantly sailed up the bay to Annapolis.

Soon city church spires were visible to the lookouts and then the waterfront of the city framed by the building ways of the Christopher Shipbuilding Company. Matthew noted with satisfaction that the frame of the ship being built on the ways was filled out to the level of the main deck.

When the ships arrived off Annapolis, Matthew directed the ships to anchor in the river off the shipyard and had himself rowed ashore.

Eric was waiting at the pier side and greeted his son warmly as he climbed up to the pier. "Son, do you know what day of the month this is?"

"Sure. The fourth of July, 1798. Just in time for the celebration."

"Not so. You arrived a few days too early, and I'm not talking about Independence Day."

"What do you mean?"

"Rumor has it that the Congress will pass a law by the tenth allowing you to be a privateer and to sell prizes and their cargo."

Matthew grinned. "Well, I suspected something like that. I've emptied and sold everything in the two frigates that isn't nailed down."

"You did the best you could, but the prize court will take over both frigates."

Matthew shrugged. "One is badly shot up and the other has a rotten bottom from too much time in the tropics. I wouldn't expect to get too much from them."

"What about the pretty little merchant ship out there? What does she hold?"

"Mostly rum. I took off all the gold bullion she had on board. She was headed from Spain through the Caribbean to France."

Eric grinned. "We can't let the prize court have all that rum or the ship either. I've got to plan something so we end up with both."

Eric got up and paced around, occasionally leaning over to rest his arthritic knees. Suddenly he stopped and straightened up. "By God! I've got it! I'll go over to the prize court this afternoon and attempt to delay the turnover of the ship until after the law is passed. If I can't arrange it, turn over one ship only every two days, insisting that we lack pier side space to turn over the prisoners. Then stall as much as you can."

"Yes, but they'll still get the *Circe*."

"The *Circe*?"

"Yes, that's the pretty litle ship out there. The vessel and its cargo are worth thousands of dollars. I don't think we can stall for more than five days. That won't make it."

Eric laughed. "I know it won't. In the meantime, don't go near her prize captain. I'll go out and see him before I go to court."

"What will you tell him?"

"Don't ask, and I won't tell you, and then you won't have to testify before the prize court judge if he sends for you. Just act dumb and you will be all right. Now I'm going up to see Judge 'Whiskey' Murphy."

"Whiskey?"

"Rum will do, and I'll need it soon."

"Good luck."

———

Later Eric came back, driving his horses slowly, then carefully tying them to the hitching rack.

Matthew watched him as he came in the door. "I take it you lost your battle?"

Eric grinned. "Yes, I lost the battle, but I'll win the war. Old Judge Murphy is famous for wanting either money or whiskey when he makes a decision."

"Did you try either on him?"

"No. I knew it would be a long chance." Eric smiled wickedly. "I'm going to beat him on the Circe. He can have the two old frigates."

"And you won't tell me?"

"No. You'll find out later."

Matthew shrugged. "Well, I've always trusted you, and you rarely lose."

Four days later, Matthew went to the shipyard, looked out into the harbor, and then he ran inside the office. "Father! The *Circe* is missing."

Eric took a large drink of coffee before he replied. "Well! I'll be damned!"

"Do you know something about this?"

"I'll tell you as soon as the law is passed. My scouts tell me it will be July 9th."

On the tenth the packet came in with the latest papers from Philadelphia. Eric was waiting for Matthew in his office with one spread wide on his large desk. "Look at this! The cowardly bastards finally did it!"

"Yes, but too late for us."

Eric shrugged. "We didn't do too badly. We lost the old French frigates you shot up for target practice, but we still have the *Circe*."

"The *Circe*. She's gone."

"No, she's been moved over to a pier at our yard in Chestertown. You could go over there tomorrow in the *Mary* and incidentally bring the *Circe* back renamed as a new prize. Take your daughter Ellen with you. She could begin the sale of rum which should be almost unloaded by now."

"Why her instead of Dresser? It's his business."

"Hers, too. He's in Washington on company business. Also bring back a few barrels of rum."

"All right, how did you get the *Circe* over there?"

"I slipped out at night and had a conversation with Velasquez. We made some mutual arrangements. He let a few prisoners out and let them think they had re-captured the ship. When the ship was clear of the harbor he took the ship over again, changed her name to *Ariadne,* declared her his prize as of that date, and headed for Chestertown."

"Why such an elaborate game?"

"Judge 'Whiskey' Murphy. If he hales anybody into his prize court and asks them about the affair, you can say you know nothing about it and Velasquez can say he was temporarily overcome, and the prize is a different ship. When Velasquez came to, they had ruined the compass and he had to head for Chestertown to get it repaired. Just in case, I had Velasquez give her a new name."

"All this is too complicated for me."

"That's good. I hope it will be like that for Judge Murphy, too."

"Won't he be able to untangle it?"

Eric squinted as he looked out the window at some seagulls wheeling over the boy, "Not when he's full of booze. I hope to keep him that way until this blows over.

The rum you are bringing back will be just as good as whiskey to old judge Murphy. By the way, double the amount I asked you to bring back. We should also toast our success. I don't think the Judge should get it all."

The next morning Matthew sailed the *Mary* across the Chesapeake Bay to Chestertown with Ellen eagerly pacing the quarterdeck with him. As they neared the yard they could see the upperworks of the *Circe* alongside the fitting out pier. He anchored the *Mary* and had himself and Ellen rowed over to the *Circe*. Velasquez and Matthew's older brother Kevin, who ran the yard, met them as they climbed to the deck. Both were grinning broadly. Kevin asked, "You heard the news about the new privateer law?"

"Sure, but just to make it easier, paint the name *Ariadne* on her before you let her leave. Then we'll consider her captured on this date as a prize under that name. Put it in the log that way."

"Will Judge Murphy let you get away with this?" Kevin asked.

"Certainly. Father has it all figured out. We'll take twenty barrels of rum back with us. He'll get half and we'll keep the rest. Keep some for yourself."

Velasquez grinned. "What can I have? I made this possible."

Matthew nodded. "Take all you can carry for yourself. As soon as you get back to Annapolis and get rid of the ship, I need you back aboard the *Mary*. We're going to sea again soon. Now where is Ellen?"

Kevin said, "She's over on the pier dickering with the liquor merchants, who arrived yesterday in wagons."

Matthew led the group over to the pier. Ellen was standing on a barrel talking to a group of merchants. Her skirts whipped in the breeze to reveal her white stockings and black slippers. She held a board and pencil and looked out over the men. "How much am I bid for a butt?"

One of the merchants snickered. "Ma'am, please call them barrels. You might embarrass us when you talk about selling your butt."

Ellen retorted. "This is still a butt and not a barrel. If you want to buy these get your bid in."

There was a flurry of bids; soon Ellen raised her hand and said, "Only one at a time. I've got to get this done and return to Annapolis today."

The merchant who had spoken before said, "I'll take your butt back in my wagon any day."

Matthew stepped forward and glared at him. "Get on with your business, and bid on more than one barrel at a time. I'm ready to sail."

The proceedings sped up, and bidding became general. In an hour the barrels were all sold and were being rolled to the waiting wagons.

Matthew said, "Let's get our barrels over to the *Mary* and set sail. Kevin, I didn't see you collecting your rum."

Kevin laughed. "You didn't look closely enough. One of those wagons was mine."

"Well then, all aboard," Matthew called out. "We have to catch the tide."

Early the next morning Matthew eased the *Mary* along-side the pier at the Annapolis shipyard and directed Velasquez to anchor the *Ariadne* nearby.

As early as it was, Eric was sitting in his rig with the Judge sitting tensely beside him. Murphy's side whiskers framed a red nose that had grown that way as he imbibed hundreds of gallons of whiskey. His hands shook slightly, and he had to keep a firm hold on the arms of his seat.

Murphy said in his raspy voice, "That looks a lot like the ship that escaped from here a few days ago."

"It certainly does. Must be a sister ship, but I note that the name *Ariadne* is on the stern. Don't you agree that she is a legitimate prize under the new law?"

"Well, I don't know. Isn't that the same dark-faced captain who was on the *Circe* when I saw her last?"

"That's our officer Gunner Velasquez. He was captured by the crew of the *Circe* when they escaped. He had let his prize crew go ashore except for three men. They broke out and sailed the ship south and threw him and his men over the side. Luckily the *Ariadne* had been taken as a prize just off bay's entrance by another of our ships and was being sailed up to Annapolis by a prize crew. They saw our men in the water and picked them up. Here they are, trying to dry themselves out."

Murphy snorted. "Eric, that's the biggest lie I've ever heard you tell, and you're famous for them."

Eric raised his voice. "Why Judge, you must learn to trust me. Look over there. The *Mary* is unloading your rum even now."

"Hush! Hold your voice down. I have a lot of con-stituents down here and the word might get out. Now let's get out of here."

"Could we drive up to your prize court and get an early start on declaring the *Ariadne* a legitimate prize? We're a

little short on cash, but we have plenty of rum."
    "Anything. Just keep quiet and drive fast."

Chapter 21

Three days later, after he was sure Martha was used to his return, Matthew woke up early and reached over to his wife. She awoke slowly and yawned. He caressed her with increasing intensity as she moved towards him. Then she returned his advances and helped him pull off her nightgown. She giggled as she moved closer to him. "You sailors never wear nightclothes. I like it, though."

Martha's body was still slim and lithe whereas Matthew was beginning to gain weight. Martha laughed. "You need a little exercise. I'll take you out walking."

After his blissful morning Matthew went down to the kitchen and brought up two cups of coffee and a plate of cinnamon toast.

Martha smiled as she took the cup and the toast. "Matthew, you aren't fooling me. Last night, when you told me how easy it had been to take the prizes, I knew right away what you wanted to do next."

"But I don't just want to go to sea. Under the old law money for the prizes didn't help us much. You know we've been putting all our assets into building two privateers and two fast merchant ships. All the prize money I managed to cheat the prize court out of barely paid for the shipyard's back expenses. Now we have an opportunity to forge ahead with winning a lot of prize money under the new law with little risk."

Martha shook her head. "Oh, sure, there is risk all right. You take a chance on making a lot of money or losing your life."

"I don't look at it that way. I could be run down in the street by these fast buggy drivers any day. The odds at sea are strongly in my favor."

"I don't understand."

"My ships will be far faster than any ships I'll meet. No

square-rigged frigate can come within four knots of my ships. They are also more maneuverable. They tack quickly while the frigates take minutes to turn. The enemy gunners will have a hard time keeping us in their sights. The biggest advantage will be our guns with three or four hundred yards of extra range."

"And you think this can produce victories without getting you killed?"

"I think so. The odds are so good I feel I have to use them."

Martha stretched her arms over her pretty head. "Well, I've always trusted you before and I will now."

"As far as money is concerned, we should do well. I know MacIntosh can do well with the privateer *Martha,* but as her captain, he is entitled to keep a substantial share of the prizes he takes. The owner's share is much less. If I go to sea once again, I take almost all except for the crew's share. In one or two voyages I can retire again, and our financial situation should be restored."

Martha laughed. "You aren't convincing me. Go ahead and go to sea and don't ask me again. Now come back to bed and show me what kind of a sailor you are. By the way, next time put more cinnamon on the toast."

Later, after they had dressed and gone downstairs, Martha said, "I've been saving this until I could have your full attention."

"What is it?"

"A letter from Bruce. It came when you were gone, and it worries me, although the points that concern me can be corrected. Read it."

Matthew stirred more sugar into his coffee and settled down to read the ten page letter. There were coffee and salt water spray stains on it. He shook his head. "I don't know where he was when he wrote this. Maybe up in the maintop, although he couldn't have taken coffee up there." As he read it, he frowned. "Damn!" he said, "Captain Barry had a hell of a time."

"Well, so did our Bruce. He was right there when the ship had all her troubles."

Matthew nodded. "The part that disturbs me the most is about the yellow fever. I gather there was a lot if it in Philadelphia, and Captain Barry had a hell of a time getting a crew together. They knew that the ships would be crowded and that there would be a greater chance of catching the fever."

"Yes, but for us the most important part is that Bruce didn't catch it."

Matthew shuddered. "I keep thinking about the crowded crew's quarters and the cramped facilites for the officers and midshipmen. A disease like yellow fever would have been hard to control. Listen to this:

'I tried to tell you how crowded the ship really was, but you have to see it to believe it.'"

Martha interrupted him, "The ship was huge. How could it be that crowded?"

Matthew shook his head. "I have every confidence in Humphreys, but somehow he didn't have much feel for people. He designed well and built even better but he put too much of the available living space into the captain's quarters. After that there was very little space in the berthing area for the crew, officers, and midshipmen. Bruce was crowded into a bunk and a locker the size of a very small closet. I'm glad you didn't see it."

"But he never complained."

"No, he wouldn't. But his opinion was clear when we saw the ship together."

"Read on about the part where Captain Barry had trouble getting the ship outfitted. I don't understand much about that but you will."

Matthew took up the letter again and brushed off a stain so he could see the writing better. He grunted, "That damned niggardly Congress again! I sometimes despair for our country. They depend heavily on the Navy, but they won't pay for it. Bruce says Barry had to pay for a lot of equipment from his own funds and still had to get underway with less than he needed. Bruce says he expects to have to take a prize or two to fill up on gun powder and food."

"That doesn't sound like the way a ship named *United States* should be run."

"There's more."

"Tell me what all that means about the lumber in the ship being faulty," Martha asked.

"If I believe what Bruce says, Joshua Humphreys had to use inferior lumber in certain parts of the ship when he first constructed her, but he then replaced it when he could wheedle enough money out of Congress to buy better lumber. That was an important step."

"I agree. I don't like the idea of our son sailing on a ship like that."

"I don't either, but this ship is still better constructed than any other ship in our Navy or any British or French ship twice her size."

Matthew read on down the letter. Then he laughed. "Listen to this. Bruce says he thinks the Navy is going to get better with the new Secretary of the Navy Stoddert."

"How can he help?"

"Bruce says the last items they needed to go to sea were two coils of rope and fifty pounds of butter."

"I suppose Captain Barry paid for them himself or took up a collection from the officers."

"No. Secretary Stoddert stepped in and wrote a short note to the Navy's Purveyor of Stores and ordered him to furnish them immediately."

"And he did?"

"Yes, and the secretary then wrote another short note to Captain Barry and, according to Bruce who saw the note, 'The *United States* under your command, being equipped, manned, and sound, will proceed to sea at the first fair wind.'"

"Wasn't that a bit of an overstatement?"

"Very much so, but Captain Barry chose not to make an issue of the remaining shortages and got the *United States* underway on three July, 1798."

Martha sighed. "Now we'll only hear from Bruce about the ship in his occasional letters. Bruce is not a very faithful writer."

Matthew laughed. "He'll be too busy to write."

Chapter 22

For a month Matthew prowled the shipyard pier, looking over the repairs being made to the *Mary* and the *Martha*. Astern of them the two fast merchantmen were being loaded. Dresser, helped by Ellen, worked like mad coordinating the arrival of a hundred wagon loads of goods. Eric estimated that the four ships would be ready to leave together in early September, 1798.

In the evenings Matthew and his officers sat over steins of beer at a large table in Jebediah's tavern. Matthew and Scotty MacIntosh sat on opposite sides of the largest table in the dining room with their officers alongside them. Dresser and Eric sat at the ends to referee their discussions of the strategies and tactics Matthew said he expected to be used when they went to sea.

Matthew said, "Our first mission will be to escort our merchantmen to Havana Harbor and back. We will also cover their loading at Matanzas Harbor. In the meantime, our two privateers will form a scouting line north of the coast of Cuba to the coast of the Florida Keys. We will be looking for French ships coming back through the Florida Straits, from the coast of Mexico and South America, and bound for France. Juan Castro may be able to use his spies to alert us to French ship movements and even their convoys sailing north from Mexico and the coast of South America. They will have to pass through the one hundred mile wide gap of the Florida Strait."

Jarrell asked, "Why do we want to concentrate on ships bound northward?"

Matthew laughed patiently. "Ships coming south carry trade goods from France. We don't need them or the cargo they will be carrying because they aren't particularly valuable. We'll take them for the value of the ships if they come by. What we really want is the gold that ships going north will be carrying from Mexico and the countries of Central America."

Jarrell shook his head. "Thanks. I think I missed that point."

Matthew nodded. "Now if we should capture any prizes, we'll put prize crews aboard and keep them close by us. That way we can use minimum prize crews and assume they won't be retaken."

MacIntosh agreed, "And going north you'll use your usual scouting line?"

"Yes. It will give us a good chance. We'll move our track east several hundred miles to have a good chance at intercepting French ships coming north from the passages between the Caribbean islands. I don't think we will miss many."

"I don't think we will either," MacIntosh said, his fair hair standing on end and his reddish complexion deepening as the excitement of the discussion rose. "Although I'm sure the French will bunch their merchantmen into convoys and provide escorts."

Dresser couldn't remain silent any longer. "We'll take those bastards like we did before!"

Matthew smiled. "Dresser, calm down. You won't be there, although I wish you could be."

"Why not? Ellen could run this business."

"Yes, she could, but I want you to stay here and prepare for expansion. We want to handle exports and imports for everybody in this area. Juan Castro has promised to give us a virtual monopoly on trade with Cuba and in nearby Spanish ports. This could be a great opportunity for the export-import business."

Dresser whistled. "That kind of success will make us all worth millions."

Jebediah shook his head. "That's chicken feed. If we take a couple of French merchantmen loaded with Spanish gold, we'll all be rich."

Matthew pushed the plates aside and cleared the middle of the table. "Enough. We know how to find the bastards. Now let's talk about how we're going to take them."

Dresser leaned over, his eyes sparkling with interest. "Ah, now we get into tactics. Just like the Greeks and Romans."

Matthew sighed patiently. "You've been reading Thucydides again?"

"Certainly," Dresser said, "The old man was pretty good. He wasn't much of a deep-water sailor, but he was a brilliant tactician. By the way, Captain, you haven't lost a ship or a man yet."

Matthew grinned, "True, but I just tricked people. Now we'll have to do this the hard way. By now the French know all about us, so they'll be on the lookout. Now, MacIntosh, start the discussion. I talk too much."

MacIntosh's color faded as he thought about Matthew's words. "Right," he said firmly. "Let's get to it." He put four gravy boats in the middle of the table. "We don't need to rehearse our scouting line. I presume our two fighting ships will be in the middle of it, and on contact our two merchant ships will take position astern of us.

Matthew agreed, "So far, so good. Now we come to the hard part. You can bet each small convoy will be escorted by one French 36-gun frigate or the equivalent."

Velasquez frowned. "Nothing bigger?"

"Maybe, but probably not. They can't afford bigger ships on this kind of duty."

MacIntosh sighed. "All right. This means the two of us will have 40 guns against their 36 on one frigate. About the same number of guns."

Velasquez grunted. "You forget our new guns will out-range theirs by at least three hundred yards, maybe more. This is very important."

MacIntosh smiled eagerly. "Thank you. I feel better. Then how do we use these guns to our best advantage?"

Matthew let them go at it and Jarrell finally answered, "Simple. Always use our speed. One ship takes position parallel to her on her beam and out of her range and then peppers her. Our other ship comes up astern and uses her bow chasers to rake her stern, while remainig outside the range of her stern chasers. Try to disable her steering gear and kill her officers." Matthew continued, "Let's use two of these gravy boats as our ships. Let the dish of biscuits represent the enemy ship."

Jebediah grinned. "Throw me a couple of those biscuits before you sink them. I'm getting hungry."

Matthew picked up two biscuits and tossed them to Jebediah. "Be patient. We'll stop soon. Now you'll notice that we must keep the enemy at the center of our formation. Our positions must always beat to each other a right angle. That way one of us will always be firing a broadside and the other will be able to peck away at her vulnerable stern."

Jarrell broke in, "And eventually she'll get mad and turn toward the ship astern of her."

Jebediah said, "I get it. Just like dogs and a bear. We'll reverse roles and give her another dose of gunfire."

Matthew nodded. "One of us will always be in a position to pound her beam and the other will hopefully always be in a position to destroy her steering gear and the officers on her poopdeck. Even if our second ship is ahead instead of astern, destroying their fore sails will limit her ability to tack and change course."

Jebediah grabbed two more biscuits. "This will be a short-lived bear."

Matthew said, "All right, enough for tonight. Let's meet tomorrow night and consider some other situations. After another week of discussions we won't even need to communicate. It will just be routine."

Linthicum interrupted. "But, Captain, you need to make provision for the unexpected. Let me make up a simple signal book something like the one the British use. Just numbers keyed to a hundred or so commands and reports. We can provide simple flags, one for each number."

Matthew laughed. "More Thucydides?"

"No. The British signal book you captured years ago. Great reading."

"All right. It's your job. Have it and the flags ready in a week. We leave soon."

———•———

Matthew knew he wanted to leave as soon as possible, and he tried to give Martha as much of his time and attention as he could for a week or so. She seemed to sense his mood and tried to return his affection and thoughtfulness, but at the end of a week she sighed deeply at breakfast one morning. "Matthew, it's no use. Leave as soon as you can and come home as soon as you can. I don't want you around like this."

———•———

On the tenth of October, Matthew eased the *Mary* off from the pier side using a gentle offshore wind to move her. One by one the other ships followed and soon the little flotilla stretched down the middle of the Severn River and out into the bay.

Martha sat in Eric's carriage and watched the ships until their sails disappeared. She said little, and Eric remained silent, too, sensing her mood. When they could no longer see the sails, she patted Eric's knee softly to avoid irritating his arthritis. "Eric, please take me home."

At the house, she got down swiftly, signalling that Eric did not need to alight and hand her down. "Eric, thank you. By Sunday I'll be in a better mood. Please come by for dinner and bring your wife and daughter."

Eric nodded. "Of course. I look forward to it."

Chapter 23

On the quarterdeck of the *Mary*, Matthew watched the spires of the numerous Annapolis churches as long as he could make out the figures of Martha and Eric. Then he sighed and turned his attention to the four ships of his flotilla. In his eyes, and in the eyes of the sailors on passing ships, they were a beautiful sight. Their graceful lines showed that they were built for speed. Even the merchantmen looked fast, and there were few differences in the hulls of the four ships. The merchant versions sat lower in the water, burdened by hundreds of tons of cargo, but they still looked, and were, fast.

All four of them were two-masted schooners, carrying two large main course sails and a jib and a trysail forward. All sails were capable of being shifted from side to side for tacking quickly with a minimum of two men per sail to shift them. The square-rigged frigates of the day, by contrast, were slow and clumsy, and required several dozen men to accomplish the same task of tacking by changing the angles of a dozen sails.

The one drawback of the schooners' narrow hulls was their inability to mount two large guns back to back. Matthew and Velasquez, with the help of Matthew's younger son, John Paul, had rigged the guns to be mounted alternately, so that there could be minimum interference with the inboard tackle of the guns of the other battery. The greater range of the new American guns permitted them to use smaller weight guns, although the *Mary's* guns were almost as long as French guns of greater weight. The stronger bronze could withstand more powder pressure.

Matthew strode up and down the main deck, patting the pommels of the guns as he passed their powerful-looking inboard ends. He was satisfied they would do their jobs. They had aleady proven themselves on the previous cruise.

Matthew reached the forecastle and turned to look astern at the other ships. Before they departed, he had directed them to form in an echelon on his quarter, and they were now a thousand yards apart to port.

The sun glinted on the patches where their woodwork was newly varnished, and Matthew thought the appearance of the ships was a tribute to the workmanship of the Christopher shipyards. He chuckled, "Even old Joshua Humphreys couldn't do better," he said to himself.

The next day they left Chesapeake Bay. Days like this were known locally as "Blue October Days." The sky was a deep cloudless blue, and the air was dry and warm. They were beautiful days.

Matthew watched the passing shores of the wide mouth of the bay entrance, and when he was sure they were well clear of the southern cape, he turned to Jarrell, who had the watch "Bring her to south." The *Mary* swung quickly, and the others, still in echelon to port, swung in wide arcs and regained relative position.

When he was sure they were in proper alignment, Matthew flipped open the signal book Dresser had made, ran his finger down the columns to the entry "Form scouting line distance ten miles," and noted the number following the entry. He turned to Jarrell and ordered, "Hoist number 58."

The newly sewn flags fluttered up on a halliard, and in a few minutes the other ships hoisted the same number, indicating they received and understood the signal. Matthew grinned and turned to Jarrell. "Haul down the signal, and watch the other ships. Now we'll see if it works."

Then the ships hauled down their flags, and the others began to take their positions in line at ten miles distance from each other.

Matthew grinned. "I hope they'll do it."

In half an hour they were in positions in a wide scouting line. Jarrell scratched his head and smiled. "I'll be damned!

It worked."

Matthew laughed. "Of course it did. The British have been using it for years, and even the American Navy has a simllar system."

Jarrell nodded. "Now we have one."

The little flotilla sailed south for eight days without sighting any other ships, and on the beginning of the ninth day, they sighted the entrance to Havana Harbor through the low morning clouds. Matthew watched their two merchantmen enter the harbor and then turned north with his two privateers to form a scouting line across the Florida Staits, between the Keys and the north coast of Cuba.

For four days the horizon remained clear and nothing was sighted except flying fish and schools of porpoises. Matthew began to get discouraged, but on the fifth day the lookouts shouted, "Sail ho! Dead ahead!"

Without waiting for an amplifying report, Matthew grabbed a long glass and raced up the ratlines. After a thorough study of the approaching sails, he clambered down quickly. Velasquez, who had the watch, was waiting for him when he hit the deck, "Well, Captain?"

"I think our patience has paid off."

"How, sir?"

"All are French ships, judging by the cut and color of their sails. A frigate in the van and five merchant ships following. There is no doubt in my mind that they are all French."

"Now what do we do?"

The first move is up to the frigate. She'll make up her mind soon."

The minutes crawled by, each man and officer on deck holding his breath. Then, after five minutes, the French merchant ships turned away, and the frigate stood on at full speed, all sails still set.

Jarrell yelled, "Dammit! The French merchant ships are getting away!"

Matthew shook his head. "No. We'll have time to over-take them before dark. Now let's get on with this fight. First things first. Beat to quarters!"

The young boy drummer, who doubled as Matthew's steward, flailed away at his drum, with a maximum of ener-gy and a minimum of skill, and the crew ran to their quar-ters.

Jarrell assumed the watch. "Captain, what do you want to do next?"

Matthew interrupted his close examination of the oncom-ing frigate and said over his shoulder, "Just like we discussed in Jebediah's tavern. Take us to the south to pass her just at the limit of our gun range, MacIntosh will hold back and take position just at maximum gun range and then he will reverse course and hold position ahead of him."

"But, Captain, she's headed toward MacIntosh."

Matthew nodded patiently. "She'll turn away soon and return to her convoy. Don't worry. Her captain will be afraid we'll pass him and get to his ships. It will all work out, and soon we'll have her in our vise."

Matthew raised his glass and resumed his examination of the French frigate. "Three masts. 36 guns. Fast for a square rigger, but slower than we are by four knots. She'll take for-ever to tack. The French will never learn. Neither will the British. She's flying a French flag proudly, but mark my word, it will come down within the hour. Ah, there. The Frenchman is reversing course, and we're on our way."

Jarrell was listening only partially, focusing all his atten-tion on maneuvering the ship. Now that the frigate was headed away from them, the four knots slowly brought the *Mary* up on the port beam of the frigate, and MacIntosh, who had been dawdling ahead of the frigate, now reversed course and sped up to maintain position astern of her.

In half an hour Matthew judged he was close enough to the Frenchman to fire his starboard battery. He turned to Velasquez, "Fire a ranging shot. If it is good, commence fir-ing the whole battery."

Velazquez turned to the nearest gun, which he had carefully positioned himself, and ordered it to fire. The gun boomed, and all those on the quarterdeck watched the flight of the ball. It landed just at the waterline of the ship.

Matthew turned to Jarrell. "Just a hundred yards closer, please."

With the schooner rig it was easy to make the adjustments. Four men previously detailed to man the sails quickly made the necessary changes and were soon back on their gun stations.

Velasquez took one last look at his battery. The gun crews were all waiting, guns elevated to the maximum, 45 degrees.

Velasquez ran to the guns and made a last minute adjustment to the quoins, small wooden wedges which, when driven into the carriage supports with a wooden mallet, changed the elevation of the gun and hence the range. Pulling them back decreased the range.

Velasquez ran back to the quarterdeck and nodded to the captain. "All ready, sir."

The captain returned the nod. He had complete confidence in the gunnery officer and never questioned his decisions or recommendations. They made a good team.

The gun captains checked their guns, making small adjustments as the range changed. Velasquez ordered another single gun fired, and the shot landed on the deck of the ship. Velasquez immediately ordered, "Commence firing!"

Then the Frenchman began to return fire. Smoke billowed out from her port battery, and those on the deck of the Mary waited anxiously. Then all of the French balls fell four hundred yards short and sank harmlessly into the sea. The crew cheered and waved derisively.

Then the *Mary's* first salvo landed, and pieces of rigging flew into the air. The crew was too busy reloading their guns to cheer again, but Matthew could tell they were happy.

Matthew turned to look at the *Martha*. Her bow chasers first salvo had landed on the poop of the frigate, and Matthew could see mass consternation on the French ship's quarterdeck. Several officers were down, surrounded by men tending their wounded.

Just as Matthew predicted, the French ship changed course as quickly as she could and headed for the *Mary*.

Matthew shouted to Jarrell, "Head away from her!"

Velasquez immediately manned the stern chasers and began to fire them at the oncoming frigate.

Out of the corner of his eye, Matthew could see that the *Martha* had changed course to parallel that of the frigate and was now firing her full starboard battery at the plunging Frenchman. By now her rigging was in a shambles and at least half of her sails were badly holed. The foremast was leaning at an angle as the French sailors fought to brace it and keep it from falling over the side.

The balls the *Martha* had put in her quarterdeck had taken their toll, and the frigate was having trouble steering. Suddenly she veered to starboard and the sails began to luff, losing the wind.

"She's gone," Matthew said, "Now we'll just pound her until she gives up."

After three more salvos the French colors fluttered down, and the ship began to wallow in the sea without steering or wind in her remaining sails.

Matthew grabbed his signal book and ran down the list of phrases. "Send the *Martha* numbers 47 and 63."

The quartermaster ran up the flags. Jarrell asked, "And what does that mean?"

"Take prizes and proceed to Havana Harbor."

"And what do we do?"

Matthew put down the signal book. "These ships will be here when we come back. Continue on as we are and as soon as we are clear of the French frigate head for the merchantmen."

Matthew picked up the long glass and looked at the French merchant ships, just barely hull down over the horizon.

"I make them about eight miles away. We'll overtake

them well before dark. I'll need five prize crews. Jebediah will head one and he'll be in charge of all of them if I have to leave them alone. Jarrell, appoint four of our best petty officers to be temporary lieutenants. They will be safe under our protection and can manage with minimum prize crews. Now let's crack on all canvas and herd them into Havana Harbor."

Chapter 24

The *Mary* fairly leaped ahead. The French merchant ships were all square-rigged and were limiting their advance to the speed of the slowest ship. The sun was still well up when the *Mary* became close enough to fire a shot at the last ship. It fell close aboard, near enough to make the merchant ships lower their colors and lie to.

In an hour the five prize crews were firmly in charge and began to sail their ships obediently behind the *Mary* like a flock of ducklings. They joined the *Martha* circling the French frigate like a hen caring for a wounded chick.

"Looks like a damned barnyard!" Jarrell muttered.

MacIntosh's prize crew and a group of petty officers had made essential repairs, and he signalled that he was ready to proceed.

Early the next day all the French ships were herded into Matanzas Harbor. Matthew sent a messenger by boat to all the ships ordering the prize masters to submit a manifest to him   by sundown.

At dinner in his tiny cabin, Matthew read over the manifests, passing them to Jarrell, Jebediah, and Velasquez in turn. There was a lot of whistling and an occasional gasp of surprise as the group read the lists.

When he had finished, Matthew gave the others a few minutes to read before he rose and stared out one of the stern ports. Then he turned to the group and called to his young steward. "Port for all hands!"

When they had glasses in hand cigars lit, he grinned at the officers. "We did it! There are several million of dollars in gold alone in those ships. Add to that the value of the resale of the barrels of rum and the ships themselves and we will all be rich."

Jebediah began to smile widely, but then he sobered. "Yes, Captain, but it's all useless just sitting in this harbor. It will only become valuable when and if we get it to Annapolis."

Matthew put his cigar out in his port glass. "You're right, but I think we'll make it. We sail in a few days. I think we'll leave the crews on the privateers approximately intact. I'll use prize crews from our merchantmen and one gun crew from each of our privateers on the frigate. That should give the prize crew on the French frigate the ability to fire two guns. Even if all they can do is make some noise, any French warships we encounter might think we have three warships. That would be a formidable force and hopefully enough to scare them off. I think we'll go a hundred miles to the east to avoid the usual track of French ships bound south."

Jebediah, still full of port and the spirit of their recent success, complained, "But, Captain, we won't intercept any ships out there."

Matthew laughed. "Just so. This time we don't want to take any risks. We just want to get home safely."

The next morning, tired of watching the stevedores work in the heat of the harbor, Matthew went ashore in Matanzas to see Juan Castro, who had come to visit Matthew's flotilla. After he had downed a cup of Cuban coffee and lit up a cigar, Matthew looked around the well-furnished office. "Juan, you seem to have offices all over Cuba."

Juan laughed, his teeth flashing. "I do. I make the rounds frequently. I have to remind the natives who is in control and who is their benefactor."

"Do you go around by horseback?"

"Oh, no. I go by my own fast-sailing vessel. It can even beat yours. By the way, can you sell me anything from the prizes you took?"

"No. They were full of cargo destined for France. Just barrels of rum and a little gold."

"I've got too much rum already. Good luck."

The next day Matthew was still impatient and decided to

visit Jebediah to see how he was doing with his prize command.

Jebediah was ready for him at the gangway wearing his sword, and with a brace of pistols in his belt. After Matthew had saluted the flag and asked for permission to come aboard, he stopped and looked around the weather deck.

"Damn!" he said. "For a ship that was beaten up so badly it's in good shape."

Jebediah grinned. "You'll see the ship's crew working about the deck. I've let most of them out of confinement during the day. There are a few old diehards that I've kept in the brig. Most of those you see are young and eager, and they hate the French Navy and even France. They ask me every day if they can become American citizens."

"And what do you tell them?"

"Maybe after the war is over. I explain what our country is all about and where most of our countrymen came from. I say most came from countries where they wanted to be free."

"Do you point out that our country will probably give them a grant of land out on the frontier?"

"Oh, yes. They want to know all about that."

Matthew frowned. "You'll have to tell them they'll probably be prisoners until the end of the war. They might even be exchanged for American prisoners."

"They won't like that. They don't want to go back to France and have threatened to kill themselves."

"Well, tell them we will do all we can to keep them in our country."

Jebediah said, "Thank you. Your words will help me to control them. Right now I keep them all locked below at night except for two ten-men watches who willingly trim the sails and steer the ship. As you can see, the petty officers have done a lot to repair the ship. The cook can take care of us. He was stolen from a good French restaurant by the captain, and I have offered him a job when I can get him into our country."

"And the wounded?"

"Below. The surgeon can take care of them, and I let him bring all of the ambulatory wounded topside as much as possible."

Matthew smiled. "Well, you obviously have control of the situation. I'll see how I can help the other prizemasters."

"You don't need to. I held school for them on the way south. They are pretty much running their ships just like I am running this one."

Matthew sighed. "I hope you never go back to your restaurant. I'll need you as long as we have ships at sea."

Jebediah laughed. "Maybe, but I think all of the women back in Annapolis are missing me. Old Jebediah can't keep them all happy for long."

Three days later the merchant ships completed loading, and the flotilla sailed out of Matanzas Harbor bound for Annapolis.

The weather was moderate, yet Matthew kept searching the sky, particularly at morning and evening, for signs of hurricanes. The sky stayed clear and the barometer remained steady.

Between looking at the sky and the barometer, Matthew made frequent trips to the tops to join the lookouts. This time, unlike other trips, he did not want to sight sails. Only one passed to the west, and Matthew resisted the urge to try to take it. The fortune he had already captured was too great to risk. Matthew chuckled to himself and pulled out a piece of paper on which he had worked out a noon sun sight. On its back he scribbled from memory the amount of gold his prizes held. Then he added the amount he expected from the rum and finally a conservative amount from the sale of the prize vessels. These figures were very conservative. Still, the sum was staggering. Then he tried to determine his share as half owner of the two privateers and captain of one. The result of his calculations was still tremendous. He sighed contentedly and thrust the paper deep in his pocket.

Jarrell, who had the watch, grinned and asked Matthew, "Are you trying to calculate the value of our prizes?"

Matthew laughed. "Yes, but I'm only guessing. No matter how far off I am with the total, you are still a rich man, and I hope you won't retire. I'll still need you, and you will be a captain soon."

Jarrell nodded. "I won't retire. I like this life, and as long as I go to sea I want to go with you, or at least on one of your ships."

Matthew leaned on the bulwark and watched the flying fish. In a few minutes he turned to Jarrell. "At least one more voyage for me. This is too easy."

Jarrell pursed his lips. "It has been, but one unlucky shot could end our time at sea, even end our time on earth."

Five days later the group of ships entered Chesapeake Bay. Matthew heaved a sigh of relief, and most of the officers and men in the group felt the same way.

The next morning Matthew sailed ahead and maneuvered the *Mary* alongside the shipyard pier. He didn't like the idea of not arriving with the rest of his men and ships, but he felt he had to arrive early to make arrangements for adequate berths for such a large number of ships.

Eric bounded aboard, ignoring his arthritis. "Where the hell is everybody else? Did you lose them?" His eyes were wide and anxious.

Matthew slapped his knee and roared, "Don't worry, old man, the rest are just over the horizon." He pointed down the bay.

Eric shielded his eyes and followed Matthew's finger. "My God! The horizon is full of sails!"

Matthew shook his head. "Wait a few minutes, there are more."

Eric grinned. "You mean there are even more than I can see?"

"Six prizes total. One is a frigate and the others are merchantmen full of rum and gold."

Eric tried to do a brief jig, but his knees hurt, and he had to compromise by uttering a loud "Yahoo!"

Matthew laughed at him briefly. Then he said, "I'm here early to help you plan for berthing all these ships."

"Well, we can moor the *Martha* outboard of the *Mary*. We will have to put our two merchantmen at the fitting out pier in order to give Linthicum a chance to unload and sell their cargo. The prizes will have to be anchored off the shipyard until we can clear them through the prize court and then find space somewhere else."

In an hour the other three Christopher ships were moored, as arranged by Eric, with the prizes anchored nearby.

Using the cargo manifests Matthew gave him, Linthicum put Ellen in charge of unloading the company merchantmen, and he jumped in a nearby boat and headed for the nearest prize. In an hour he was back, a grin clear across his face. "This is fabulous." he shouted. "I never saw so much gold and rum all in one place."

Eric asked, "You mean you counted it all in an hour?"

"Oh, no. I just looked at it."

Matthew nodded to Eric. "Let's get this to the prize court. My men are very eager for their shares."

Eric said, "So am I. This will ensure the whole family's financial security for decades. We've done it!"

Matthew pulled at his chin. "I think we should send a couple of barrels of rum to old Judge 'Whiskey' Murphy."

"What for? We don't owe that old bastard anything, and the law is clear," grumbled Eric.

"Maybe not, but you never know when you will need a favorable ruling on some obscure matter. The new prize law hasn't really been tested yet."

"I'll take care of it. Now get along and see your wife. I have been summoned to appear before the Marine Committee of Congress. I'll be back in a week to tell you what they want. In the meantime, young John Paul is doing a fine job of running this shipyard and Kevin is running the other. John Paul will come after you if he needs help."

Chapter 25

Eric dropped Matthew in front of his house. "Son, stay home for a week as I told you to do. Don't sneak back to the shipyard. They got along all right for a month while you were gone. In the meantime, I'll take care of the congressional business as well as what goes on in the yard."

Matthew laughed, but it was obvious he was uneasy. "I promise, Father, I'll see you in a week."

Matthew ran up the front steps and flung open the unlocked door. Martha was in the living room, and he crushed her in his arms. After a few minutes, Martha pushed him away and laughed, "Let me get my breath back."

They talked throughout the afternoon, Matthew trying to recount all the events of the cruise. Martha could hardly take in the magnitude of the prize amount and asked him to tell her more about it later. "Right now I have something of more importance." She pulled a letter from her pocket. "I had a letter from Bruce just after you left. I've read it several times, but it's so good and so full of news I'd like to read it to you. This will take some time, so pour yourself a drink."

Matthew poured half a tumbler full of Scotch and added some water. Martha noticed what he was pouring and commented, "I thought you liked rum for lunch."

Matthew shuddered, "I've seen enough rum to last me a lifetime, although I'll enjoy selling it."

Martha shrugged. "Good. I prefer the odor of Scotch on your breath anyway. Somehow it seems more manly, and I never did like rum."

"I don't think you took in what I was saying about the prizes, You are now the proud owner of at least a million dollars worth of rum."

Martha gasped. "But I don't want any of it. I told you I preferred Scotch."

Matthew laughed. "We don't have to drink any of it.

Linthicum and Ellen will take it over and sell it, and we'll get the money."

Martha rolled her eyes. "All right. Let's talk about that and the gold later. Now for this letter. "I'll start with the best part. It's signed by Lieutenant Christopher."

Matthew leaped up, almost spilling his drink. "By God! He did it! I'm very proud of him. Now go to the start and tell me all about how he did it."

Martha grinned. "Now keep quiet, and I'll read it all to you, but a little at a time."

"Dear Parents:

This has been a big voyage for me. As you can see, I am now a lieutenant. Captain Barry just told me after he returned from Philadelphia that the appointment is now permanent. Poor Lieutenant Sherrod will have to leave the Navy because of his injuries.

"You will receive this early in 1799. Of course we were at sea for months before I could mail this to you. In October we were at sea off the New England coast. A very big storm came up suddenly. The locals call these storms 'noreasters'. Although we were well reefed down, the captain did not expect such gusts of high velocity winds, and the mizzen mast and its yards and rigging came crashing down. I had the midshipman's watch and Lieutenant Sherrod had the deck watch. Of course Lieutenant Sherrod was standing near the binnacle at the base of the mizzen mast, and the wreckage fell directly on him."

Matthew interrupted, "It's the large mast just forward of the binnacle. It's the after-most mast."

Martha said, "I understand, and I'll go on.

"I sent the messenger below for the captain, and I grabbed an axe and started freeing Lieutenant Sherrod from the tangle of lines and spars. I had cut away most of the wreckage when the captain stormed up on deck. 'Why didn't somebody call me sooner!' he shouted over the shrieking of the wind.

"'There wasn't time, sir,' I said. 'This just happened.'

"The captain looked at the work I had done and seemed to approve of it, 'What? You mean you did all this in the time since you had me called?'

"I said, 'Yes, sir. Lieutenant Sherrod is caught under the wreckage, and I almost have him out.'

"'Keep up the good work.' Barry shouted. "He took over the conning of the ship and gave orders to ease her.

"In a few minutes I had poor Sherrod unbound and had two members of the watch drag him loose. I could see that he had a bad fracture and was in severe pain. I made an improvised splint out of a long glass and tied it to the leg with some pieces of the log line I cut loose. Then I had two members of the watch carry him below to the surgeon.

"'Well done, lad! the captain said again over the terrible roaring of the wind. "You might as well take over the watch now. I expect to appoint you as acting lieutenant in Lieutenant Sherrod's place.'

'But sir, he'll be all right.' I said.

"The captain shook his head. 'No. He won't ever go to sea again. I've seen a lot of such cases. The Navy will beach him.'

"We managed to get through the storm and the night and I was glad to see my relief come on deck.

Matthew got up to pour another drink and interrupted, "I'm very proud of him. He had all the qualities necessary to make a good naval officer. I knew it was just a matter of time before he was rewarded."

Martha looked up from the letter. "Yes, but there's a little luck in it. He had to have the opportunity to show the captain what he could do."

"Believe me, for a good man there will always be an opportunity. If it hadn't been weather it would have been battle. He would have come through."

The maid came in and announced, "Luncheon is served, Ma'am."

Martha nodded. "Thank you, Sally. Matthew, let's eat now. I'll finish the letter over coffee. The rest of it is mainly housekeeping."

"Well, that would be more interesting to me. If you'll give it to me I'll finish it later."

"Oh no you won't. I want to read all of it over again so we can both enjoy it."

———————

Over coffee Martha picked up the letter and read more passages. She continued.

"The food is passable. The captain does his best to keep it from spoiling, but we stay at sea too long, and that's beyond his control. The captain's a strict disciplinarian, but very fair. I hope to run a ship like that if I last that long."

Matthew grinned. "Just as I taught him. He'll make a good captain."

Martha kept reading,

"The midshipmen's quarters are still miserable. Crowded, dirty, and poorly ventilated. The officer's wardroom and bunkroom are very little better. My so-called stateroom wouldn't make a chicken very happy. I suppose I'll get used to it some day."

"Anything else?" Matthew asked.

"Not much more."

"Good. Let's go to bed."

Martha laughed. "Just like a sailor."

Matthew got up and stretched. "I won't rush you. I'll be home for a week, and I hope to see a lot of you and the family in that time."

Martha raised her eyebrows. "Well, that's not like you. I thought you'd be back to work tomorrow."

Matthew grinned. "It was Eric's idea."

"Good for him. I'm glad you're listening." She got up and stretched, too. "We're both stretching. Are we tired or just getting old?"

Matthew reached out and caressed her long, black hair. "You're not getting old. You're still the beautiful girl I married."

She laughed. "You sailors are always full of flattery, but I like it."

He took her in his arms and caressed her, gently at first, gently, and then with mounting intensity.

She pushed him away. "All right, I'm convinced. Let's go to bed. I'm not tired either."

Chapter 26

A week later, Matthew was dressed in his working clothes. He ate an enormous breakfast and kissed Martha goodbye. Though he was in a hurry to get back to the shipyard, he could not help but to thoughtfully admire the streets of Annapolis. As he went south along gently sloping Church Street, Church Circle was behind him and ahead was Market Square, where produce merchants and fishermen gathered to barter their wares. From nearby waters they had taken oysters, crabs, and occasionally a few lobsters.

Walking along Church Street, he noticed that at least half of the dwellings were being converted into stores and offices. Soon the name Main Street would be more appropriate. Matthew turned short of Market Square, leaving behind him the odors of fish and produce, and walked a short distance northwest along the waterfront to the shore side building of the Christopher Shipbuilding Company. The buildings were identified by modest signs over them with their names outlined in gold letters.

Matthew thought about the many offers from real estate brokers to buy the property. Commercial development was expanding around them, and the property was urgently needed for development. Matthew had asked some of the same brokers about buying a large tract of undeveloped land across the harbor in an area called Eastport. A much larger and more modern shipyard could be built there, and the profit from the sale of the old shipyard would finance the whole deal. Moreover, the workmen could relocate into nearby living areas where houses were less than half the price of the ones they were forced to occupy now. Matthew sighed, resolving to broach the subject with Eric soon. It would have to be done, but it might have to wait until the war was over.

He turned into the entrance to the shipyard and hastily

scraped the bottoms of his shoes, removing the street dirt and horse dung, and went into the office.

He knew Eric had come back from Philadelphia yesterday. His trap was in front of the shipyard office, the horses already munching nosebags full of oats.

Matthew pushed open the door and bounded in. But instead of the confident, ebullient father he usually was, Eric sat behind his desk in a morose fog, nervously fiddling with a pencil.

Matthew demanded, "What's wrong with you?"

"It's not just me. It's you, too," Eric said. He gestured disdainfully at a pile of official-looking documents sitting at his elbow. He pushed the papers toward Matthew. "Take a look at these. Read these documents from top to bottom, and you may lose some of your breakfast."

Matthew picked up the top paper and began to read it. Halfway through he threw it on the floor. "My God! They can't do this! It says the Congress has confiscated the *Mary*, and she is now the U.S.S. *Mary* of the American Navy!"

Eric laughed hollowly. "There's more, but they have generously given you a hundred thousand dollars for a million dollar ship."

"Peanuts!" Matthew growled. "I'll take them to court, or I'll have them horse-whipped."

"Won't do you any good. You'll find a check there, for a hundred thousand dollars, and if you'll endorse it I'll deposit it. Now read the other papers."

Matthew picked up the second paper and soon threw it on the floor with the first one. "This is my commission in the Navy as a Captain."

Eric nodded. "Keep going. The next paper gives you command of the *Mary*."

Matthew sighed, "That's a little better. And my officers of the *Mary*?"

"Look at the next papers. They are commissions for Jarrell, Jebediah, and Velasquez as lieutenants."

Matthew laughed. "This may be the only ship ever officered by a bunch of extremely wealthy men."

Eric stirred and seemed to be about to come out of his black mood. "Speaking of millions of dollars, I've spent several days when I wasn't in Philadelphia squaring away Linthicum and the prizes and their contents. First, I dropped off several barrels of rum at Judge Murphy's home to assure we'd get favorable rulings."

"Favorable! The law is plain. We own all of the ships and their contents," grumbled Matthew.

"Plain or not, the Judge can cause trouble or delay. Now he's in our pocket. Dresser took ten wagon loads of gold bullion to the bank. As a matter of fact, he had to use all five banks in town to take it all. Their vaults are full now. As far as the rum is concerned, merchants are coming in wagons from as far off as Wilmington. The news of our auction has travelled like a forest fire on a dry day. We'll have to take paper money or checks, which is just as well, because there's no room in the banks to store coins."

"And the prisoners?" asked Matthew.

"Gone to a prisoner of war enclosure on the edge of town. They belong to the Navy. By the way, Jebediah reported that one of the prisoners on his prize had escaped and seems to have gotten ashore. Do you know anything about this?"

"No, I'll talk to Jebediah about it."

"And the ships?" Eric inquired.

"We'll auction them at the pier next week. The Navy may want the frigate just as she is. By that time the banks should have transferred some of the gold and may have room for coin." Matthew thought for a moment before continuing, "How about dividing it up? The crew is probably getting anxious."

"Well, the rules of prize are fairly simple. I'll have to clear the results with Judge Murphy. You, as half owner of both privateers and captain of one, get a very large share. I'll do all right as half owner of both ships, and the officers and crew get somewhere near a million for each officer and half a million for each member of the crew."

"Now they'll all want to go ashore and buy a farm," said Matthew.

"Well, the crew of the *Martha* might be able to, but the crew of the *Mary* are, like you, members of the U.S. Navy, and they'll be going to sea with you."

Matthew shook his head, "This is the damnedest arrangement I've ever heard of. Martha won't believe it."

"You'd better go ashore and start trying to explain it to her. Stop by the tailor and buy some epaulettes for your old uniform if it will still fit you and Martha hasn't thrown it out."

"I will, but first I'm going out to see Jebediah to ask about this escaped prisoner."

———◦———

Matthew had himself rowed out to the prize ship commanded by Jebediah. After an exchange of pleasantries and the gossip of the town, Matthew asked, "What happened to that escaped prisoner?"

Jebediah grinned. "I don't rightly know how he got out or even got ashore. I guess my crew had relaxed too much. After all, they had been a little tired, and the French crew seemed to be subdued."

Matthew nodded in agreement. "And the man who escaped. Who was he?"

Jebediah smiled. "I hope you won't get into this matter too deeply."

"No, but I'd like to know what's going on. Judge Murphy may get wind of it and cause trouble. What was his name?"

"Well, if you insist, it was Pierre Aignol."

"Ah, the light dawns. Someone you knew in particular?"

"Well, yes. The French chef, er, cook, I told you about."

"And how did he come aboard this ship as a mere cook if he's so good you call him a chef?"

"He told me was a chef in a well-known Parisian restaurant. One night the captain went there to dinner and was so pleased with the food that he asked the chef to come to the ship as his personal chef. The man said he refused, but that night an officer and four men came to his apartment. They bound and gagged him and hauled him to the ship. I suppose you'd say in England he was 'pressed.'"

Matthew said. "I'd call it more than that, but I understand."

Jebediah sighed. "Thank you."

"I suppose he's being confined in the kitchen of your restaurant?"

"Well, as a matter of fact, he's already cooking, and I'm sure he won't leave."

Matthew laughed. "Please wait at least a week before you announce that you've imported a well-known French chef." He got up and stretched. "Well. I guess we have covered the subject. I'll see you ashore soon."

"Please bring your wife by for dinner in my restaurant."

Matthew nodded, "With pleasure, but I'll wait a week, too." He had himself rowed ashore and walked home. All the way he thought about the actions the government had taken. He was disgusted and angered as he stalked through his front door.

Martha started to hug him, but she stopped and stood back. Her eyes widened. "What on earth is wrong?"

"You're looking at a newly commissioned captain in the United States Navy with no uniform and a ship that no longer belongs to me."

Martha took him by the hand. "Come sit down. I think we both need a drink before lunch."

When they were seated and Matthew had gulped half of his drink, Martha said, "Now tell me about this captain thing."

"I've been drafted by the Congress into the United States Navy as a captain." He threw the commission on the floor. Martha picked it up and read it.

"I understand this, but why? And what about not having a uniform? Your old lieutenant's uniform is hanging in the attic. It has a lieutnant's insignia on it, but it should still fit you."

"Would you take it to the tailor this afternoon and have captain's epaulettes put on it? I'm supposed to be in uniform tomorrow."

"Now what's this about losing your ship?"

"Well, I'm most disturbed about that. The *Mary* has been drafted too, and it is now the U.S.S. *Mary.*"

"But will you still command her?"

"Fortunately yes, and my officers are now lieutenants in the United States Navy. The members of the crew are also enlisted men."

"Well, aren't you a happy bunch?"

"Not really. We all wanted to go ashore and spend our money. We're all rich but we can't spend any of it."

"Well, you waited long enough to tell me. I might as well spend most of it."

"You won't. You never waste anything."

"Well, there's something else I might do, and we might as well start tonight."

"And what might that be?"

"I want to have another baby."

"What! You're too old, I mean, I think you shouldn't."

"First, I'm not too old, but on second thought I'll wait until the Navy is finished with you."

Chapter 27

The next morning Matthew shrugged into his slightly tight uniform, now sporting captain's epaulettes. He looked at himself in the mirror and shuddered. "Either see the tailor or eat less," he muttered.

Martha looked over his shoulder and pursed her lips. "Try cutting back on food first," she said.

Matthew turned toward her, grinned, took her tightly in his arms, and kissed her goodbye fondly.

She sighed as he released her. "I don't like this," she said. "I trust you when you are in command of your own ships, but now you have to do what someone else says to do, and I don't know if that's right."

"I know, and I don't like it either, but I'll find some way to survive."

Matthew strode down Main Street toward the *Mary*, which was lying quietly at the pier side. He felt a little odd in his captain's uniform, but after all, he had been a lieutenant for many years walking down the same street. Some citizens raised their eyebrows, and also raised their hats. He nodded pleasantly and touched his cap in salute.

When he reached the *Mary* at her berth, he was still preoccupied and bounded up the brow without looking up at her rigging as he usually did. Jarrell met him at the top of the brow and looked at him quizzically. A young sailor, sweeping the deck nearby said, "Cap, you forgot to salute the colors." He pointed to the American flag flying from a staff aft.

Jarrell colored and turned abruptly to the sailor, "Dammit, Harrison, don't call him Cap! He's Captain Christopher to you from now on."

Matthew looked at the sailor and grinned. "My fault, Harrison. We all have to get used to a lot of things. By the way, you need a shave and a haircut and some clean clothes, or better yet a uniform."

"Ain't got the money, Cap. By the way, you should have looked aloft, too. We're flying a Union Jack forward and a commission pennant from the main truck above. Guess that makes us a regular man-of-war."

"It does Harrison, but all that does is buy us a ticket. Now we have to show the Navy we can fight. In a few minutes I'm going to address the crew to tell you all how rich you are. Then you can get some uniforms."

"Okay, Cap."

Jarrell was shifting from foot to foot, obviously still angry. "Harrison, how many times do I have to tell you to address the Captain as 'Captain'?"

Harrison picked up his broom. "All right, Lieutenant Jarrell. I'm not really a hayseed. I was just having a little fun. When I put on the uniform I'll act like a real sailor." Harrison brought his broom to an imitation of present arms. "Good morning, Captain. Permission to go back to work?"

Matthew returned his salute. "Permission granted, Harrison. I'll see you at quarters soon."

Jarrell frowned and scratched his head. "What's this quarters business, Captain?"

"I know you are new to the Navy business, Jarrell. I'll do my best to break you in. In the merchant navy, quarters is where the crew lives. In the Navy it means that too, but it also means we are all to assemble topside in ranks for muster and instruction. On big ships they go to quarters every day at 8 a.m., or 0800, as we will have to learn to call it. We won't do that. Maybe twice a week. For the first time have the word passed to 'Go to quarters.' The crew will be puzzled, so tell the officers to have the men assembled in two ranks on the weather decks, and I'll take it from there and give the necessary instructions." He looked at his watch. "Make it at 0900."

At 9 a.m. Jarrell had his boatswain pass the word to assemble, and the crew struggled to their first quarters, shepherded by their officers. One or two were in uniform, but the others were still in civilian clothes. When they were in approximately straight ranks, Jarrell said, "I think they are all here, Captain. I realize I will have to furnish the other lieutenants with muster lists."

"Yes, as the senior lieutenant aboard, in the Navy you will be called the Executive Officer."

Matthew stepped forward and cleared his throat. The crew, quieted, and Matthew began, "Men, as you know, the *Mary*, myself, and all of you have been drafted into the Navy."

There was a loud groan in the rear and a voice said, "You tell 'em, Cap."

Harrison, in the front rank said, "Lieutenant Jarrell, that wasn't me."

Matthew quickly said, "Now that we are all in the Navy, we will have to make some changes. In the first place we have all been drafted for the duration of the war. We have no choice."

The voice in the rear groaned again.

Jarrell strode up and down in front of the ranks, but he could not locate the culprit.

Matthew went on, "If you leave the ship at any time without my permission, you will be considered 'absent without leave' and confinement will follow. If you desert permanently in time of war, you will be tried by a general court martial, and you may be hanged."

The voice in the rear rose again, "Ouch!" it said.

Jarrell's head went up, "Whoever said that, keep quiet."

The voice said, "Okay, Loot."

Jarrell frowned. "And don't call me that. I'm Lieutenant Jarrell."

"Okay, Loot Jarrell."

Matthew put his hand over his mouth to hide a grin and sought safer ground. "About your prize money." There was a loud roar, and when it died down the voice said, "Let's hear it for the money, Cap."

Jarrell's voice rose irritably, "Don't call him 'Cap'. It's Captain!"

The voice said, "All right, Loot. Let's have it, Captain."

Jarrell started to walk to the rear of the ranks to find the culprit, but Matthew stepped in. "All right, men, I expect you to learn naval language soon, but in the meantime, let's get back to the prize money. Prize is the same word in any organization."

The voice in the rear rose again, "All right, Captain, let's have it."

Jarrell nodded. "That's better."

Matthew regained the initiative quickly. "Prizes are being processed rapidly by Eric Christopher and Dresser Linthicum. You should all be paid most of your money by the end of the week."

"How much, Cap?"

Jarrell frowned. "Maybe you won't get any if you don't learn proper naval phraseology."

"I got it, Loot. How much, Captain?"

Matthew said quietly and patiently, "About a million dollars for each of the officers and half a million dollars for each of the men."

A shout went up and turned to cheering. When it died down Matthew said, "I hope you will all put most of it into one of the banks."

The voice in the back said, "Cap, you ain't no true sailor. We've got other plans for it."

Jarrell had given up temporarily and he stayed quiet, glaring silently at the area in the rear where he thought the heckler was standing.

Matthew thought he had the crew in hand now, and he went on, "You will all be given shore leave, which means permission to go ashore, half at a time. I hope you'll all come back promptly the next day at noon, with your beards neatly trimmed and your hair the same, although you may keep it long if you keep it clubbed. I hope you will all be uniformed by then and that you'll all be clear-eyed and sober."

Laughter broke out, and when the noise had subsided the voice said, "Hell, Cap. Most of us will be falling-down drunk."

Velasquez could see that something had to be done, and he moved to a position behind the rear rank. Matthew spent a few minutes instructing the crew and reminding them of the dire punishment for anyone who didn't return. Then he said to Jarrell, "Please dismiss the crew and join me in my cabin for a cup of coffee."

A few minutes later, Jarrell came to the cabin and tossed his new uniform cap on the small settee. He shook his head and sat down heavily. "Captain, I don't think we will ever be able to make this group into a Navy crew."

"Don't worry about it. They are all fine young men who recently fought very well. All this is new to them. They are just feeling their oats."

"And besides, all that money. I'd like to spend some of it myself."

"Well, go ahead. Set up a watch bill with one officer aboard at all times. Since you are making up the watch, go ashore yourself tonight. Would you like to join us at our home for dinner."

Jarrell laughed, "Thank you for your kind invitation and I hope you'll repeat it a little later. Like our sailors, I'd like to live it up first."

"Do you have any particular girls in mind?"

"About half a dozen now, but I'll narrow the choice down. I'm not in a hurry."

"Watch yourself. They may be in a hurry to tie down a rich and handsome young fellow like you."

After coffee Matthew prepared to go see Eric at the shipyard. As he left the ship, he was careful to salute the officer of the watch and the colors. Harrison, still working on the deck, said in a loud voice, "I see you learned, Captain."

Matthew grinned. "So have you, Harrison. You learned to call me 'Captain'. Remember what I said at quarters."

Chapter 28

Matthew, becoming more comfortable in his captain's uniform, walked all the way to the waterfront, enjoying meeting civilians on the street. He strode into the shipyard office and sat down opposite his father.

"Good morning, Father," he said.

When he saw his son in uniform, Eric laughed loudly and slapped the table top. "Good morning. I thought there was a riot going on aboard the *Mary*. What was happening over there yesterday?"

"I was just having the crew assemble at quarters for the first time."

"I hope you'll do better soon. Maybe you ought to turn Jarrell loose on that crowd. Every time he tried to get them in shape you let them up."

Matthew grinned. "An old naval trick. Either the captain or the executive officer has to be a bastard and the other gets to be a good fellow. Now Jarrell is being the bastard. Next week we'll trade roles and the crew will be so confused they'll fall into line without knowing it."

"Good ploy, but basically they are all good men trying to find out how much they can get away with and how far they can push you."

"Not far, and it will all work out. I've seen a lot of naval life, and I can predict what they'll do. Although, I don't think any captain ever had the task of commanding a crew worth so much money."

"I don't envy you."

"Sailors just want enough money to have a good time ashore. I'd appreciate it if you'd warn the police. This will be a hell of a town for two nights."

He advised, "The best thing you can do is to get them in uniforms and out to sea. Then you can whip them into shape."

"I don't worry about whether we can fight or not. I know about that. We've licked everybody we have come up against."

"You do it with cleverness, speed, maneuverability, and gun range. When you come under the command of someone else you may be in trouble. He won't know how to use your talents or your ship's abilities. Let's just hope you don't end up under the command of some moron."

"That worries me, but not too much until I find out who will be my senior."

Eric frowned. "You won't have long to wait." He pushed an official-looking paper over the desk. "This came in on the packet this morning. Read it."

Matthew scanned it and then read it thoroughly again. "Who's Commodore Ephram?"

"Some political hack put in command by the Congress of a small frigate named the *Confidence*. He will have his ship, yours, and two smaller schooners yet to be named. He will be in command because his commission was issued two months before yours, and having four ships under his command entitles him to be called commodore."

"I am ordered to join him and his ships off the entrance to the Chesapeake Bay in a week, and then he is to take us to the Caribbean."

The next week was a frantic period for Jarrell as he tried valiantly to get the crew sobered up and into shape. First he had them all scrubbed to remove the evidence of barroom floors from their bodies and uniforms. They were all put in new or clean uniforms, and Jarrell ordered them to cut their hair short. There was a near riot until Jarrell was reminded that the captain had promised long hair would be permitted if it was neatly clubbed.

Their initial time ashore had taxed the abilities of the police force and nearly emptied the supplies of the bars. Eric did his usual duty behind the scenes by dropping off barrels of rum at the homes of the police force members. There was still plenty of rum around that had been purchased from Linthicum earlier.

At the end of five days, Matthew mustered his crew carefully and said a hasty goodbye to Martha, who was standing on the pier with Eric.

Eric sighed with relief. "Never thought I'd like to see that ship go to sea. I don't think the town members or the police force could hold out much longer."

Martha ignored his comment and said to Eric, "I don't like this one bit, but he does look handsome in his uniform."

The crew, in spite of heavy hangovers, succeeded in doing their usual skillful job of getting the *Mary* underway, and Martha waved a last goodbye to Matthew. He saw Eric pass a handkerchief surreptitiously to Martha and knew she was crying in spite of her erect posture.

He turned his attention to the set of the sails, and when he looked back, Martha was gone.

Early the next morning as they passed out of the Chesapeake Bay, the lookouts reported three sails in a group off the entrance. Matthew ordered all sail put on and had soon closed the gap. The lookouts reported that a numbered hoist was flying on the frigate, the largest of the three ships. "58," they reported. Matthew looked up the numbers in a navy signal book he had been given before they left and declared, "Captain report on board."

Matthew said, "Lieutenant Jarrell, please call away my gig."

"Gig? You mean the starboard pulling boat?"

Matthew said patiently, "That's the one. In the Navy it's called the gig."

Jarrell managed to get the pulling boat in the water and alongside in spite of some heavy seas. Matthew clambered down the bobbing sea ladder and the coxswain did his best to hold the boat alongside while Matthew jumped in. Then he managed to push it off without sinking the boat. The crew were all skilled watermen and soon were pulling well together. Matthew noted that some of the crew with long hair had failed to club it properly and wisps of it were hanging out. Two had their jerseys outside of their trousers, although they were reasonably clean. He made a mental note to smarten up the crew later. In the midst of large seas was not the appropriate time to instruct them.

Matthew noticed that the stroke oar was Harrison, now shaved and reasonably fitted into his uniform. Obviously, as stroke oar, Harrison had been chosen by Jarrell as one of the most competent seamen, in spite of the tiffs between the two. Matthew said, "Harrison, how are you getting along with Lieutenant Jarrell now?"

Harrison was puffing from his exertions, but he managed to reply between strokes. "We get along just fine, Captain. He's made me a petty officer."

"I don't think he knows yet that petty officers are now entitled to wear distinctive badges on their sleeves. I received a shipment of badges, and if you'll stop by my cabin I'll give you yours. I think it's very handsome."

"What's it look like, sir?"

"An eagle in flight. I think you'll like it, and the men under you will respect it."

Harrison laughed. "I maintain discipline because I can lick them all. They wouldn't dare disobey me."

Matthew pointed to the coxswain sitting next to him in the stern sheets of the boat. "Could you lick Varian here?"

"Don't have to bother to find out. He's in a different gang, the deck group."

Varian, a husky farmboy, laughed. "I don't think so, Captain, but we won't have to find out. Lieutenant Jarrell has made me a petty officer as coxswain of your gig."

"Good, drop by and pick up your badge. Now be careful with your approach alongside the flagship. They should throw over a sea painter for your bow hook to pick up."

Varian brought the boat smartly under the lee of the flagship, and a sea painter was thrown over. When the boat was riding comfortably to it, Matthew clambered up a bobbing sea ladder and nimbly threw a leg over the bulwark. He looked up. An officer wearing a captain's uniform was leaning over the bulwark looking at his boat, but when Matthew looked at him, he stared back sternly. Matthew saluted the colors flying from the gaff, and announced, "Captain Christopher of the *Mary*, sir. Permission to come aboard?"

The captain returned his salute with a little more stiffness than necessary and said, "Commodore Ephram of the United States Ship *Confidence*. Please follow me to my cabin." He turned on his heel rudely and left Matthew in his wake.

In the cabin, Ephram gestured to a small settee and said, "I can offer you some coffee, but I don't recommend it. My steward is a dolt."

Matthew muttered, "No, thank you."

Ephram sat down and stared at Matthew. "Captain, I am to be addressed as Commodore Ephram."

Matthew nodded. "I understand, sir."

Ephram cleared his throat ostentatiously, squinted his eyes, and went on, "Your gig is a disgrace, I hope your ship is in better shape. As you leave you will see what a good ship should look like."

Matthew bristled. "I wasn't aware that your jurisdiction over me applied to such matters as administration. I thought we only fought together."

"It does very definitely, and I'll show you my orders if you think otherwise."

"That won't be necessary," Matthew continued apologetically. "I'm afraid I can't keep up with you in matters of appearance yet. We've only been in commission ten days."

Ephram sniffed. "I don't accept any excuse, sir. I hope you fight better than you look."

Matthew compressed his lips and asked, "And you have been in action?"

Ephram screwed up his face unpleasantly. "That's not

your business, sir. I'll fight with the best of them when we're brought to action, and I expect you to close the enemy promptly when I signal you."

"Sir, I hope you will take into account the advantages of my ship. She is faster and more maneuverable than any ship we will meet, and her guns will outrange any French ship by four hundred yards."

Ephram sniffed again, and Matthew wondered if he had some disease of the nasal passages. The commodore said disdainfully, "I don't expect you to hide behind those, er, qualities. All I want is for you to close the enemy promptly when I signal you. Can you do that?"

"Well, yes sir. But you will be wasting my advantages. I have taken every ship I have met so far, some bigger than this ship, including two French frigates. I haven't lost a man yet."

"I don't care about that. It sounds like you weren't close enough. I'll change your habits." Ephram rose abruptly. "Now if you'll excuse me, I want to get back to inspecting my ship." The commodore led the way to the quarterdeck and ordered the officer of the deck to bring the *Mary* gig alongside. The coxswain did his customarily skilled job, although the officer of the deck had allowed the ship to lose her lee.

Ephram looked over the side at the crew of the gig. He shook his head disdainfully and turned to Matthew. "I hope your boat is in better shape when I come over to make my formal inspection in about two weeks."

Matthew was livid, and in clipped tones he said, "Permission to leave the ship, sir?"

Ephram nodded and returned the salute so crisply that he almost knocked his cap off.

Matthew tried to keep his face straight and clambered over the bulwark. When he was seated in the stern sheets next to the coxswain, he said, "Varian, to the *Mary* please, where disorder reigns, but I'm beginning to like it."

Varian raised his eyebrows but said nothing. To his crew

he said, "Out oars."

When the boat had been shoved away from the side, he said, "Give way together."

The boat spun rapidly and headed for the *Mary*. Matthew leaned over the stern and spat carefully in the direction of the flagship. He was sure Ephram was watching, but he didn't give a damn.

———•———

Back on the quarterdeck, Matthew gestured to Jarrell. "Please follow me to my cabin."

Jarrell asked in a puzzled tone, "Is something wrong?"

"Oh, yes, we've 'caught a tartar,' as the saying goes."

"You must mean Commodore Ephram. What's wrong?"

"He's a nut, and one of the worst kind."

"How so?"

"There's a saying that a captain who doesn't realize his ineptness as well as his stupidity will kill himself, and in doing so may bring disaster to those around him."

Jarrell said, "One of those. Now what will we do?"

"Protect ourselves. When he does something to kill us all, we hope we will have enough speed left to get away. In the meantime we'll see him over here for inspection in about two weeks."

"But we'll probably be fighting by then."

"That won't matter to him."

Chapter 29

Matthew sat in his small cabin looking glumly at the opposite bulkhead. He could not get the face of Commodore Ephram out of his mind. He felt that somehow he would bring tragedy to them, and although he did not know how it would happen, Matthew felt that it was inevitable. Matthew knew he would have to find a way to save his ship when the inevitable crisis occurred, but he felt he would not be able to save Ephram himself, his ship, or even the rest of his command.

Suddenly there was a loud and urgent knock on his door. "Come in," he said.

The messenger of the watch opened the small door and poked his head in. "Captain, the officer of the watch reports that the Commodore's flagship has gotten underway and has hoisted a signal meaning 'Form column in order of seniority.' The officer of the watch has headed for his position, second in column."

Matthew roused himself. "Thank you. Tell him I will be right there."

Matthew was still morose and moody when he reached the quarterdeck, but soon the fresh sea air and the sunshine restored his normal composure.

He watched the ships maneuvering and approved of Jarrell's handling of his own ship. "Just right," he said to Jarrell. "I wish I knew a little more about the two schooners that appear to be taking their proper positions."

"We know something," Jarrell said. "When you were visiting the flagship, I sent Velasquez in our other pulling boat over to the *Bee* and the *Newark*. He wanted to borrow some spare parts for the gun flintlocks. While he was over there he found out quite a bit about the ships."

"So?"

"The *Newark* was built in Philadelphia and her captain is

named Fernald. She has 12 guns."

"And the *Bee?*"

"The *Bee* was built in Portsmouth and her captain is named Stimson. She also has 12 guns and the two ships are very similar in capabilites."

"Was that bastard of a builder in Portsmouth named Langston mentioned?"

"Yes. Captain Stimson wasn't very complimentary. He didn't like the design or construction of the magazines, and he spent a lot of time arguing about it. He said the *Confidence* was built that way, too, and their magazines were even worse. He said he thought her captain didn't seem to know enough about naval construction to object and he's glad he's not serving on that ship. He's sure the magazines are unsafe."

"Are you sure ours are safe?" Matthew asked.

"I am, because I know you inspected them frequently when they were being built. Now you seem to be down there most of the time."

Matthew laughed. "I feel like I have been, but I think it will be worth it."

"And you were sure the *Ranger's* magazines were safe?"

"I helped Captain John Paul Jones put the *Ranger* in commission in that yard. We had to overcome the shoddy work of that yard every month, and the yard's owner, Mister Langston, cheated the government in every way he could."

"Captain Stimson said Commodore Ephram had been mayor of Portsmouth until six months ago. He told his congressman, an influential member from Portsmouth, that he felt he could help the country more if he could go to sea as a captain of a ship, and the one being built at the shipyard seemed to be ideal for him. Langston, the builder, put in his oar for Ephram, obviously thinking that the mayor could repay him, and the arrangement was made."

Matthew said, "Thus we have this clown to deal with."

"I hope this doesn't become a circus."

Matthew nodded. "Let's all hope we can survive this fiasco somehow."

By now, the ships of the flotilla had formed up and Matthew lost interest in their movements. He walked over to the binnacle and pulled out a chart of the Atlantic. He traced Comodore Ephram's apparent course toward the Caribbean Islands.

Jarrell, looking over his shoulder, asked, "Where is he going?"

"I think he's headed for Mona Passage. You'd think he'd tell his captains where he's going."

Jarrell sneered. "That's one of the first rules of command. Keep your subordinate commanders informed of your actions."

"Right. I guess we'll discover his plans after a few days of sailing time on this course. He'll have to go somewhere in the chain of islands known as the Greater Antilles. I hear the new Secretary of the Navy has set up a series of flotillas at the choke points in the islands to intercept French ships."

Jarrell cleared his throat. "The new secretary, Stoddert, has done a lot. Captain Stimson told Velasquez that the Secretary had placed representatives at each shipyard and naval supply point. Stimson thought this would stop the criminal activity in the Portsmouth shipyard.

Matthew banged his fist on the binnacle. "That's only the start. He'll have to check carefully on his own representatives to see that they aren't bribed by the likes of Langston."

"Did he approach you?"

"No, but he did bribe another officer."

"And did you find him out?"

"Yes, but he was well protected by big congressmen, and Captain Jones just laughed it off."

"Well, you had no options then."

For four days the Commodore maneuvered his flotilla using flag hoists. Matthew and his watch officers tried to keep up with the orders from the signal book, but sometimes they made little sense. Fortunately one of the smaller ships seemed to misunderstand the most, and Commodore Ephram's wrath was focused on it. Matthew shook his head. "Thank God! I couldn't cope with a 'slap your wrist' session from that bastard for very long."

A few days later they arrived at the Mona Passage, the strait between the islands of Santo Domingo and Puerto Rico. For several days they patrolled the broad expanse of blue water between the shores of the tropic islands adjacent to it. Soon Commodore Ephram became bored and the signals flew overhead. The flagship's halliards looked like colored ribbons. Jarrell, the glass glued to his eye, read off the numbers. Matthew ran down the columns in the signal book as Jarrell sighed, "The hoists are addressed to us."

Matthew knew what they said even before he looked them up. He swore quietly. "We will be inspected at 0900 tomorrow."

Jarrell looked puzzled." We've never been inspected like this and certainly not at sea when combat is imminent."

"When we joined he inspected me and my gig and said we were both terrible, and the ship would be inspected within two weeks. He's right on time."

Jarrell swore. "I still don't know what it means. We're at sea."

"It means the Commodore will arrive at 9 a.m. tomorrow. We must have our decks shining, our rigging tarred, our crew freshly shaved and lined up in clean uniforms. Then I still don't know just what he wants. Maybe I should have inspected his flagship to see how she satisfied him."

"Damn! Are we being examined for appearance or fighting ability?"

"Most of the review will be of the uniforms and cleanliness of the ship. I don't think he really knows how a ship should fight. We have to go along with what he wants and try to be prepared for it."

Jarrell did his best to put a "shine" on the ship and her

crew, and just before 9 a.m. the next morning, he watched anxiously as the commodore's gig approached. The ships had been anchored in the lee of Puerto Rico.

Matthew noticed Jarrell's concern and advised, "Don't let this bastard get to you. We know we are very good at fighting. We don't care how we look."

Still, Jarrell paced while Matthew stood stolidly, occasionally leaning on the bulwark. The gig came up to the sea ladder, and the bowhook fished out the sea painter and secured it to a cleat. As the boat settled back on the sea painter, Commodore Ephram rose slowly and gingerly made his way forward to the bottom of the sea ladder.

Matthew, peering over the bulwark, suppressed a grin as the Commodore stumbled slightly over the foot of an oarsman, but, after glaring at him, he righted himself and started a slow climb up the bobbing ladder.

Matthew drew back and took his post opposite the gangway. Commodore Ephram's head appeared in the opening followed by his upper body. Slowly, Ephram grabbed the sides of the gangway and stepped onto the deck. He looked down and a sneer spread over his face, but he managed to remember to say to the officer of the deck, "Permission to come aboard, sir?"

Jarrell, who had the deck, returned his salute and said crisply, "Permission granted, sir."

The Commodore looked back at the deck again, and his sneer returned, even broader.

Jarrell whispered to Matthew, "Jesus! This will be a helluva day."

Chapter 30

The first thing Matthew noticed about the Commodore other than his sneer was his uniform cap. It's cover was very clean and probably starched, and it sat exactly on the center of his head. Slightly too high to stay on in a fresh breeze. Exactly even. Not even the slightest inclination, either fore or aft or to the side. "Almost inhuman," Matthew thought. He shook his head and tried to focus on the business at hand, but it was difficult. Every time Matthew looked at the Commodore, his mind wandered to the cap, marveling at its absurd perfection and wondering if it would blow off.

Ephram continued to glower at Captain Christopher.

"Well, are you ready?" he asked. "You look like you're a mile away."

"Yes, sir, I'm ready. Please follow me."

Ephram cleared his throat loudly and said, "I don't follow you at any time. You will always follow me. I wish to see your crew. From here they look slovenly. I'll start with the officers."

The officers were ranged in front of the crew on the quarterdeck. Ephram passed down their front, examining each one in detail. For each one he had several comments, "Cap crooked. Shoes dirty. Trousers too long." The litany was endless, and it worsened as he shifted to the crew. The enlisted men were not perturbed. Each man, after Ephram, had passed him, tried to refrain from smiling as the commodore threw out a continuous stream of adverse comments. After he had passed a man or two down the ranks, the individual sailors broke down and mimicked his mannerisms. The officers shook their heads, trying to suppress the actions of the crew, but they paid little attention.

After the Commodore finished and stood back, he shook his head dolefully and began a loud tirade, "Disgraceful! Awful!" He turned to the Captain. "I'm coming back in two weeks and if there is not a radical improvement, I'll report this condition to the Congress." Then he paused. "I have never seen even a barnyard worse than this. I wouldn't even stable my horses in it."

Jarrell gritted his teeth, became red in the face, and opened his mouth to speak, but Matthew laid a hand on his arm and Jarrell subsided.

Matthew appeared to be resigned, but he tried to salvage the situation. "Now, Commodore, I hope you'll inspect our guns and their rigging. They are the best in the world, and we're proud of them."

Ephram shook his head. "I can see from here they are poorly kept and as dirty as your decks. I've had enough. Please call my gig."

The commodore asked for permission to leave the ship without looking Jarrell in the eye, and Jarrell, lips compressed and voice barely controlled, said, "Permission granted, sir. Your gig is alongside."

The gig was rowed away. The boat crew was not as skilled as the crew of the *Mary's* gig, but all the members of it were smartly turned out in horizontally striped jerseys, black tarred hats, and spotless white duck trousers.

Matthew watched them row away and said, "They look like a bunch of mechanical toys, but they can't row worth a damn! They're not even rowing together."

Jarrell had regained his composure. "We ought to challenge their gig to a race. Ours could beat theirs by a mile."

————

For a week the flotilla patrolled the Mona Passage without sighting as much as a small sailboat. Only the tropical birds came out from the adjacent shore, and porpoises and flying fish were sighted.

Jarrell gritted his teeth and said to Matthew, "One more week and the Commodore will be over to see us for another inspection. Shall I turn the men to?"

"No. Don't bother. I have a premonition that we may never see the Commodore again."

Jarrell shook his head. "You're imagining things."

———◦•⊸———

On the tenth day after the disastrous inspection, the lookouts shouted out, "Sail ho! Four ships dead ahead!"

Matthew couldn't wait. He grabbed a long glass and climbed up to the foretruck. "Where away?" he asked.

The lookouts pointed to the four ships' masts, just barely peeking over the horizon. Obviously they were headed for the Mona Passage. Matthew clapped his glass on them, watching them steadily as the masts grew to white sails. "French," he said.

The sail area increased rapidly as the two groups closed each other. "Two square-rigged frigates, about thirty-six guns each, and two square-rigged merchantmen."

The approaching Frenchmen had obviously seen them too. Both groups were on opposite courses approaching each other. Matthew wanted to examine the other group closely before they committed themselves, but the Commodore decided to plunge ahead, and he did. As the groups came over each other's horizon, the French commander decided on evasion and reversed course.

Jarrell said, "The bastard is chicken. He has two 36-gun frigates to our one frigate of 24 guns. He has the advantage."

Matthew nodded. "He should think so, but I don't. The only problem for us is our stupid commodore. If he ignores our advantage and abilities and tries to board these two heavier ships, obviously well manned, we're done. If we are ordered to close on one of those, we won't last half an hour. He might hold out for an hour and the two schooners will just be bystanders."

Still, Ephram's flotilla had a four knot advantage over the French, held back by their slower merchantmen. In two hours Ephram's group was in gun range, and the *Mary* was able to open fire early and even hit one of the frigates. The salvos of both the French and the *Confidence's* were well short, so the shots from both ships rose in geysers of tropical water.

The *Mary's* fire was increasingly effective, and some of her balls landed aboard. Matthew hoped the Commodore would learn a little from it and leave the *Mary* at longer range. Instead the quartermaster shouted out, "Signals flying on the flagship, sir, 'All ships close and board.'"

"Damn!" Matthew said. "Now we're in the soup. We'll have to continue to approach. Stall as best you can. Change course frequently to open our alternate broadsides and throw off their aim."

The *Confidence* bored steadily and directly toward the French frigate nearest her. "That makes the other ship our target," Matthew shouted. "Head for her and keep on stalling as long as you can. Maybe fate will help us."

Chapter 31

Fate was slow in helping. As the *Mary* made a turn to avoid salvos falling dangerously close, a ball penetrated the port bulwark. It bounced off a gun carriage, overturned it, and crashed out the starboard bulwark. Splinters from the bulwarks flew in all directions, and a dozen men fell to the deck, writhing with wounds from the splinters. Blood spattered the deck and men screamed in pain.

Matthew felt a severe blow to his left leg and fell heavily to the deck. The pain in his thigh was intense, and he clenched his teeth to avoid crying out.

Jarrell noticed that he was down and ran over to him. "Captain! Are you all right?"

"Hell, no," Matthew gasped between clenched teeth. "I think I may have lost my left leg. It feels like the end of the bone is sticking out."

Jarrell knelt beside him and cut away the trouser leg. He looked carefully at the thigh. "That's not a bone end. It's the end of a huge splinter, deeply embedded in the large muscle of the thigh. Fortunately you aren't bleeding badly. I won't try to remove it because bad bleeding might start. I'll call the surgeon to take care of you."

"No. Send these wounded men below to see him first. When he's finished looking after them, ask him to come up here to see me."

"Don't you want to be taken below?"

"My God, no! Ask my steward to bring a camp chair up here. I can't leave this action now. You should take command, and I'll just be here to advise you, but I won't leave."

A second salvo landed close aboard. At least three balls passed through the mainsail, tearing holes in it, but the tears stopped at heavy seams and the sail lost little wind. Matthew looked up at the sail. "See that. Another innovation by John Paul, and it works."

"I noticed there were heavy seams every three feet horizontally and vertically. Now I understand their purpose. Most sails are not sewed like that and the tears usually reach all the way to the edges of sails making them virtually useless."

Suddenly the sky was lit up from a flash as intense as a hundred fourth of July demonstrations. Jarrell looked toward the flagship, now alongside the French frigate. The two ships were held tightly together by entangled rigging and several grapnel lines that had been passed by both ships. Every time one was cut away, another line was passed.

Within seconds a tremendous boom followed, knocking down all the men on the weather decks who had been standing to watching the scene. The sails flapped furiously after the explosion but held without tearing.

Matthew grinned despite his pain. "Now you're all down here with me. Please hurry up that chair. I can't miss this."

Jarrell was the first to get up, and he looked carefully at the flagship.

Matthew asked, "What seems to have happened to those ships?" Jarrell shook his head. "I'll be damned. Both ships are burning badly. There is a column of black smoke over them half a mile high. The flame covers all of both ships. The stern of the *Confidence* has practically disintegrated. Her after magazines must have exploded."

Matthew nodded, "I don't doubt it. I told you what lousy magazine construction the Portsmouth yard does unless they are closely supervised. They want to make money and the average captain never looks below decks, and if he does, he doesn't know what to look for. I can guess some error in construction caused this terrible explosion. How badly are the ships burning topside?"

"No masts or rigging are standing without burning."

"How about flags flying?"

Jarrell laughed. "They must have burned up in the first blast. I'm sure Commodore Ephram is gone."

"Please hurry up the steward with that chair. I don't want

to miss any of this."

The young steward, pale and frightened, carried a camp chair. He looked at the scene and then shook his head when he saw the Captain. "Captain, you don't look so good."

"I'm all right, or will be. Please help me get into that chair."

The young steward shook as he lifted the captain. Matthew said, "You don't look so good yourself, young man."

"I'm not used to being on the topside in battle, sir. I'm a powder monkey, so I've always been below. After what happened, I wish I were topside."

The captain laughed, "Son, if a magazine goes up it won't matter where you are. Now you pay attention to the safety regulations I taught you and we'll all be safe. We don't want to go up like that wreck over there."

Matthew adjusted himself in his chair to minimize the pain and looked around. "I'm no longer bound by those damned signals, and I'm in charge of our force now. Wear ship and head away from that frigate that's chasing us."

Jarrell shouted out the necessary commands, and the *Mary* swung quickly to a course away from the pursuing ship. Soon the shot from the enemy ship began to fall astern. Jarrell noted it and without waiting for instructions, he changed course to put the French ship on the quarter so the port battery would bear. He shouted to Velasquez, "Keep up a heavy fire from the port battery!"

Velasquez had righted the overturned gun carriage and managed to man it with sailors from the offside battery. Now they would be able to fire a full broadside.

The first salvo roared. Matthew gripped the arms of his chair and watched the flight of the shot. At least six cannon balls struck the Frenchman. Two holed the main course sails, tearing through them from top to bottom.

Matthew was feeling better, and he turned his attention to his responsibilities. "I'm in command of what's left of this flotilla."

He turned to the quartermaster. "Bring me the signal book." He put it gingerly on his right thigh and opened it. "Send signal number 43 addressed to both schooners."

Jarrell said, "I suppose it says you have assumed command. A good idea."

"Yes. Now, quartermaster, hoist number 23 addressed to the *Bee*."

Jarrell asked, "And it means?"

"Pursue and capture," answered Matthew.

"You mean capture the merchant ships?"

"Yes. Now send to the *Newark* 'Rescue survivors when safe.'"

Jarrell remarked, "Now that you've taken care of the command business, let's get back to fighting the French frigate. She's still a problem."

Matthew nodded. "I'd say Velasquez is doing all right by himself. Take a look at the ship through the glass. All we have to do is let him alone."

Jarrell steadied the glass against a ratline and studied the French ship, now slowed radically. "We're destroying her methodically. Velasquez has her on the run. One mast down. Two main course sails out of use. The quarterdeck is clear except for several officers lying on the deck. One could be the captain. Three men are trying to get him below. About half of the gun carriages are overturned. She can't go on."

Matthew said, "Take another look at the burning ships through your glass." Jarrell swung the glass around and steadied it again, "My God! They can't stay afloat much longer."

"What makes you say that?"

All of the guns of both ships have disappeared, meaning the gun carriages are on fire, and the supporting deck beams have burned away. The red-hot guns and the flaming carriages are now lying on the bottom planks, burning holes in it. The black smoke is now tinged with white, but the white isn't smoke, it's steam. As holes have been burned in the bottom planking, jets of water have spewed up through them and turned to steam from the heat of the fire. The ships will sink in a few minutes. They are flooding rapidly."

"Good. Although I do feel sorry for all the good men who died so quickly today," Matthew said. "Now I'm feeling a little weak. Please help me stretch out on the deck, and find out if the surgeon is about ready for me."

Before Jarrell left Matthew's side, the surgeon came running up carrying a small black bag. "Why didn't someone send for me?" he asked querulously as he saw the captain lying in a small pool of blood.

Jarrell said, "I tried to, but the captain wanted you to treat the others first."

The surgeon bent over the captain and looked at the protruding splinter. "Fortunately," he said, "It doesn't seem to have damaged any major blood vessels or nerves. I'll know better when I get it out."

Matthew sighed. "Will there be much pain?"

"Yes, but I'll give you quite a bit of laudanum. You may pass out for a short time."

"Please wait until the Frenchman has struck."

The surgeon nodded. "I can do that safely. And a matter of fact, I'd like to watch some of the battle from up here. I never see much below except for crushed limbs and chests, but that's my business."

Velasquez continued to pump out salvos, and as predicted, another mast soon crashed over the side, and the colors fluttered down from the remaining mast.

"Cease firing!" Velasquez shouted, and Jarrell gave orders to close the enemy.

As they neared the stricken ship, Matthew could see the crew running to put out fires. Many wounded and dead were still lying about, and the wreckage of lines, sails, and masts cluttered the decks.

Matthew shuddered, "It looks awful."

Jarrell agreed. "But just think. We might look like that, or even worse, if the Commodore had his way."

Matthew felt himself getting weaker and decided to leave the fate of the French ship to Jarrell. He knew he would have to get help from the surgeon soon, or he would pass out.

"All right, surgeon," Matthew said resignedly. "Let's do it."

The surgeon laid out his instruments neatly on the seat of the camp chair and held a small cup of laudanum up to Matthew's lips. The surgeon waited while the captain drank. "All of it," he said sternly when Matthew tried to leave some in the cup. Then he turned to Jarrell and explained, "This will help dull the pain."

"Will it render him unconscious?"

"The laudanum won't, but the pain will."

Matthew remembered his words, and as the surgeon began his work the pain increased rapidly, and then the world turned red.

Chapter 32

Matthew slowly regained consciousness. The first thing he noticed was the wind singing in the rigging overhead. Then he could hear the waves slapping gently against the windward side of the waterline, and eventually he recognized the murmur of conversation amongst the members of the crew as they went about their business. The redness he had noticed when he lost consciousness was now a light pink gradually fading to normal. Then he noticed that the previous pain had become a steady ache, but it was much less severe.

The surgeon looked down at Matthew's foggy eyes opening slowly. He felt his pulse and looked at the bandage to see if it was leaking blood. Satisfied, he asked, "Can you hear me, Captain?"

Matthew tried to speak, but his throat was too dry to permit him to talk, so he nodded instead. He was then covered by a blanket, and something soft was folded under his head. He felt reasonably comfortable.

The surgeon anticipated his reactions. "Captain, you'll wake up quickly now. You are as comfortable as I can make you. Don't try to bend your leg yet. I've put a splint on it to keep you from pulling on the stitches."

Matthew could whisper now. "How many stitches did you have to put in?"

"About twenty. The number doesn't matter. If you pull them too early, I'll just have to put them in again. Give me five days to take off the splint, and I'll take the stitches out in a week."

"We may be in Annapolis then. How will I be?" Matthew whispered.

"Fine. You'll be sitting up in an hour and walking stiff legged tonight. I've had the carpenter fashion a cane out of a piece of the bulkhead." He grinned. "I thought the choice of materials to be appropriate because I removed a piece of the bulkhead from you."

Jarrell overheard the surgeon, but he was too tired to appreciate the surgeon's humor. "Damn! Doesn't anything bother you?"

The surgeon shrugged. "Very little. I've been in this business for a long time."

"But this is your first cruise at sea?" Jarrell asked.

"Yes, but you should have seen my operating room in Annapolis on a rousing Saturday night. I was so busy the nights this crew began liberty, as they called it, that I decided to give up my practice to a younger man and join the Navy. It might have been a bad choice."

Jarrell said, "I guess Annapolis was quite a war zone. But, up until today we haven't even had a man wounded."

"I was told when I joined up that this ship had been in several actions and never lost a man."

"Did we lose anyone this time?"

The surgeon look his head. "No, but we came quite close. Those other ships must have lost hundreds."

Jarrell nodded. "Well, you won't have to treat any of those."

"Why not? Some of them must have survived."

"Not many. The captain has ordered one of our schooners to pick up the survivors when it is safe for her to approach the burnng wrecks."

The surgeon looked puzzled. "Burning wrecks? I don't see anything over there except a few bobbing heads and a lot of smoldering wooden refuse, and there is some smoke downwind."

Jarrell spun and looked where he had last seen the hulks. "My God! You're right. They went down fast! The schooner is moving toward them."

Matthew, now fast regaining his faculties, heard the conversation. "Damn! You two stop sightseeing and get me up in this chair."

When the captain was safely wedged in his camp chair and

provided with a glass of medicinal brandy, hastily brought up by his steward, Jarrell stepped back and looked at the Captain.

"I judge you are well enough to continue to play the part of the commodore? After all, you already gave the necessary orders. Now for something simpler. Who should be the prize master for the surviving frigate?"

Matthew rubbed his head before answering Jarrell. "Why Jebediah, of course. I'm sure he's already gotten his sword, pistol, and bag ready."

"I agree, Captain, but with you on the binnacle list and Jebediah about ready to leave, we could use another lieutenant."

"You're trying to tell me something? What is it?" asked Matthew.

"Well, if I will be doing all the extra work as acting commanding officer and doing something or other as a staff officer to help you as commodore, I really think we should have another lieutenant."

"And you have a suggestion?"

Jarrell smiled. "Young Harrison."

"What! I thought he troubled you a few weeks ago," Matthew said.

Now he's one of our best gun captains, and he's the stroke oar of your gig."

Matthew almost managed a grin as he asked Jarrell, "And he has a strong, commanding voice?"

Jarrell rolled his eyes. "All right, Captain, he does have one, and you can hear him whisper from the rear rank. I might not have decided this way earlier, but now I'm convinced. I'd like to have him."

"All right. It's a deal. Tell him the promotion is temporary, and I'll try to have the Congress make it permanent. You can have the pleasure of informing him."

"Good. He won't be able to get into full uniform yet, but I'll take back his petty officer's badge and loan him a spare officer's cap."

Matthew sat quietly in his camp chair, the blanket drawn tightly about him as the sun lowered in the sky. He watched the *Bee's* boats being rowed amongst the bobbing heads. The dead were unceremoniously dragged into the boat by sailors grabbing at any part of a uniform or a limp body. The wounded were pulled in carefully, but they were relatively few.

Jebediah, his prize crew, and a group of temporary petty officers were rowed over to the French ship, to help make repairs. In the near distance, the schooner *Newark* was shepherding the two merchantmen back to the group.

When the situation seemed to be reasonably well in hand, Matthew said, "Let's close each of our schooners and deliver orders to them."

Jarrell steered a course to the *Newark* and swung around on her beam. "Captain, what shall I tell the captain?"

"Tell him, 'Proceed to Philadelphia with your two prizes. Turn them over to the prize court and then report to the naval authorities for further orders.'"

Jarrell delivered Matthew's orders in his booming voice without using a speaking trumpet, and then he headed for the *Bee,* now about to bring her boats aboard. When the *Mary* had come abeam and lowered her sails, Jarrell asked, "What shall I tell her captain?"

"Tell the captain to proced to Portsmouth and deliver the wounded to the nearest naval authority. En route, bury the dead with appropriate ceremonies. After your arrival, request appropriate orders."

Jarrell filled his lungs and delivered the message with a single breath.

Then he asked Matthew, "Now, sir?"

Matthew instructed, "Sail for Annapolis. Lieutenant Jebediah will know enough to follow you without orders. After all, he is in as big a hurry to get there as I am."

Chapter 33

The flotilla, under the commmand of Captain Christopher, sailed in column from Mona Passage generally northwest toward the entrance to the Chesapeake Bay. The French frigate was repaired in two days, after Jebediah found some spare sails and rolls of canvas in a storeroom below.

One day as both ships lay to in a relative calm, they lowered their sails, and spent the day repairing the holes made by cannonballs in the recent engagement. In the case of the *Mary* the job was relatively easy, the heavy seams already in place. On the French frigate *Medusa,* the job was more difficult. Almost all of the petty officers and all of the sailmakers had been killed by the relentless fire from the *Mary.* Fortunately the French boatswain had survived, and he pressed some of the more skilled seamen into service. Canvas was used from the damaged sails, and the spares and rolls of canvas were used where needed. By the end of the third day after their departure, the job had been completed. The flotilla was stopped at noon while the dead on the French ship were buried. A surviving French officer conducted the ceremony for fifty-three men. Each body had been sewed into a piece of used sail with a cannonball secured at its feet. At the end of the ceremony the bodies were slid over the side, one by one.

The French wounded seemed to be recovering under the care of the French surgeon, and Jeremiah, after watching him treat his patients, let him alone.

The other crew members seemed to be docile and resigned to their fate, so Jeremiah let them roam freely on the topside except for a daily required watch of ten men.

On the *Mary,* the pace to the northwest seemed to be snail-like because they had to adjust their speed to that of the slower French ship.

Matthew stopped worrying about the slowness of the passage and decided to think of it as a period of recuperation, or as the surgeon joked, a "pleasure cruise." This way he would be almost completely recovered by the time they arrived.

On the first two days his leg was painful, and on the third morning Matthew awakened much refreshed and with diminished pain. He reached for his walking stick, and slid his feet into some slippers. He adjusted the clothing he had worn continuously while sleeping because of the awkwardness of trying to remove it. Changing it had also been painful, even with the help of the steward.

He managed to stand and take a tentative step or two with the aid of the walking stick, discovering that he was surprisingly agile. He walked to the wash stand, propped his stick against the bulkhead, and filled the bowl with lukewarm water. He lathered his face and scraped off three days of beard. Then he washed his teeth with a willow twig dipped in water and salt.

Matthew took up his stick and pushed open the door to his cabin. Just outside the door the steward was approaching with a large tray.

"Ah, breakfast!" the Captain said. "I'm more than ready for it."

The steward grinned. "Yes, sir. Two scrambled eggs and a large portion of grits. The eggs may be a little ripe, but there's some hot sauce here to kill the taste if you need it."

"I'll eat anything. Just put them on the table in my cabin, and please empty the wash bowl into the slop jar. I couldn't make it."

The steward left him alone to his breakfast, and Matthew found that a little hot sauce and not breathing while he ate the eggs was all right. When he had finished eating, he felt better. He even rose without the aid of the walking stick and walked outside, taking care to stay near the bulwark in case a sudden roll upset his equilibrium.

By the end of the morning he had completed 20 laps of the weather deck, pausing to pat the pommels of the guns. Then he laid his stick aside and tried to complete a lap without it. He was still unsteady, and a passing seaman offered to bring him his stick when he noticed he was wobbling a bit.

"Thank you, son, a good idea. I might need it in case I see a passing rat."

As the seaman walked away he commented, "You look pretty fit this morning sir."

By now the other dozen wounded men were beginning to come topside, lean on the guns or the bulwarks, and take in the tropical sun. Matthew stopped by each group to chat and inquire, "How do you feel" or "Where were you when the ball hit?"

By the sixth day all of the wounded appeared topside except for one. Matthew noticed and sent for the surgeon. "Surgeon, we're missing one man up here. How is he?"

He was wounded by a large splinter. I believe he thinks he's going to lose his leg. I've used everything in my medicine chest but I can't seem to reach him mentally. He seems to need something I don't have. Can you make it below?"

Matthew nodded. "Certainly. I'll have to take it slowly and use my stick. But let's go."

The sick bay below was cramped and dark, and Matthew made a mental note to improve it. He could easily see why coming topside in the sunshine helped the other patients. He bent over the unmoving form, and the surgeon adjusted the gimbaled lantern overhead to illuminate his face.

Matthew gasped, "Why, it's you, Varian. I didn't know you were wounded. I've been out of it myself. I just noticed a man was still in the sick bay."

Varian stirred and recognized the captain. "Captain, you shouldn't be down here. I heard you got it, too. A leg, wasn't it?"

"Yes, just like yours, but not as bad."

Varian winced. "I think I'll lose my leg."

"Don't talk like that. The surgeon has hopes for you, and we'll soon have you ashore in the best hospital we have in Annapolis."

Varian sighed, "That's what I'm afraid of. In a hospital they'll take my leg right off."

"But you have a strong physique and can still recover with good care."

"Yes, but probably one-legged. Sir, I love going to sea, but I doubt the Navy will keep a crippled man."

"Don't worry about that. I'll guarantee you a job in my shipyard or even at sea on any of my ships after the war is over. You can have any job you want, anywhere, sitting or standing."

Varian grinned. The surgeon slapped Varian's knee and said to Matthew, "See, Captain, I knew you'd be good for him."

————————

On the tenth day, Matthew put away his stick. "Shall I throw it away?" his steward asked.

"Hell, no! I want to keep it over my mantel piece to remind me of my time at sea."

The steward said, "But you'll be at sea lots more."

Matthew shook his head. "I think this may be my last cruise."

Chapter 34

On the 15th of October, in the year 1800, the ships of the flotilla passed inside the entrance to Chesapeake Bay. The day before they had come far enough to the north to turn west and cross the Gulf Stream. The days of October were still crystal clear with blue skies. However, the tropical skies the ships had sailed under for the last month had turned to fall temperatures, and the crew had changed into sweaters or jackets and wool hats.

Matthew, still a little slow, wore both sweater and jacket, and wished he had something else, but after a few brisk laps he leaned on the bulwark and surreptitiously felt the wound. The hard ridges of the stitches were still there, but there was no pain, not even tenderness. He straightened up and resumed walking, increasing his pace, and he finished the lap not even breathing hard. It was time for him to go home. If he was careful, he hoped Martha wouldn't even know he had been wounded.

For a moment he thought about increasing sail on the *Mary* in order to get in several hours early, but he decided not to leave Jebediah and his command behind. He wanted all the officers and men he had served with so long to come home together.

Matthew sighed contentedly and sent for a cup of tea. The waves in the bay were warm and gentle, slapping against the port side, driven by the soft breeze. The air was dry and brisk. The perfect kind of day for fishing. He thought about Varian, lying in his bunk below, and resolved to visit him before lunch. He would remind Varian of the offer for any job he wanted in the shipyard or on his ships.

The morning went by quickly and pleasantly, and Matthew followed his steward below with a tray of soup and fried fish for lunch.

Varian was sitting up in his bunk, freshly shaved.

"You look great," Matthew said. "How's the leg feeling today?"

Varian shrugged "I'll probably lose it when I go ashore. Does your offer of employment still hold?"

Matthew nodded. "Absolutely. I can think of a dozen jobs for you, all paying ten times what you get now. Besides, you're already a rich man."

"I know. But there's more to life than money. I'd like to do something worthwhile."

"I guarantee an important job for you. I've thought of a dozen possibilities. Now eat your lunch before it gets cold. You should build your strength before you go to the hospital tomorrow. And I'll be there, too."

Back up on deck Matthew leaned on the bulwark, lost in thought. He looked up as a familiar voice rang out, "Keep that weather sheet taut!"

It was Harrison, standing his first watch under Jarrell, who looked at Matthew and grinned. When Harrison bent over to look at the binnacle, Jarrell raised his right hand and put the thumb and forefinger together in a gesture of approval.

Matthew grinned back "Oh, now youth is taking over," he said. "Maybe it is time for me to go ashore."

Jarrell smiled. "I think it is. I'm ready to take over this ship, either as a naval vessel, a privateer, or a merchantman. I've always loved her."

"I have, too. And you are the only one I'd want to turn her over to."

Harrison gave an order in a loud voice, and Matthew looked at him. "A handsome young man with a good voice," he said to Jarrell.

Jarrell laughed. "He's pretty good, but you should see and hear his sister. She's beautiful."

"I suppose she has a good voice, too."

"Yes, she sings in a church choir. Ask your wife. She's

heard her."

"Don't tell me you went to church."

"Just once, after I met her."

Matthew laughed. "And I suppose you are now going to inform me you're going to marry her?"

"I think so. I haven't asked her mother yet."

"And you know her, too?"

"Oh, yes. She runs a very nice boarding house. She's been a widow for ten years."

"I suppose you've moved into her boarding house?"

"Last time in port. Obviously I don't stay in my room much, but I like to keep one there."

"All you have to do is ask her mother, ask her, marry her, and then move into her room."

Jarrell shrugged. "That's about it, although I figure we'll need two rooms."

Matthew shook his head. "You amaze me. I knew an officer was supposed to plan ahead, but you take the cake."

"Cake, yes. Wedding cake. You will be my best man, won't you?"

Matthew smiled. "Certainly."

Harrison raised his voice to give an order, and Jarrell went aft to see what the trouble was.

Matthew watched him go. "A remarkable young man," he said to himself. "If I didn't have three fine sons already I'd wish he were my son."

Chapter 35

The next morning the two ships stood up the lower part of the Severn River, an almost straight run to the shipyard. Matthew knew Eric had counted the days and was expecting his ship home soon. He would recognize the rake of her masts and the cut of her sails. By now he was undoubtedly in his trap; racing home to tell Martha the news of the arrival. The sound of his whip would hurry up the street crossers, who would think twice about slowing the progress of Eric's horses.

Then he looked up at the *Mary's* sails, bright white in contrast with the wheat white of the French frigate following. The *Mary's* sails were expertly sewn and fitted, and the wind filled them smoothly and evenly. The French ship's sails looked like an unpressed suit. The differences in the fit of the sails separated the ships by a knot or two in speed. Add to that the slim schooner hull and the use of fore and aft sails, unlike the clumsy square-rigged ships, meant a total variance of at least five knots.

Matthew sighed, remembering the times he had heard John Paul Jones say that he always wanted a fast ship, and he wished Captain Jones could have commanded the *Mary*. Speed was her name, and she was also a beautiful ship. This would be his last voyage in her. He didn't want to leave her, but he knew it was time to go. He rubbed the polished mahogany bulwark and looked aft. "Good old girl," he said softly.

Ashore, when Eric reached Martha's house, he climbed down from the trap and ran as fast as his knees would allow to the front door. A loud knock brought an angry maid to the door to see what the noise was about, closely followed by a curious Martha, "What is it?" she asked.

"Get into your best outfit. The *Mary* is standing up the

river, closely followed by a French frigate."

"The French ship has captured him?"

"Of course not. He's bringing in the French ship as a prize."

Martha flew up the stairs and was back down in ten minutes, trailing silk, perfume, and powder.

"Let's go!" she said as she ran down the stairs... "I'm ready to go!"

"Wait for me! I'm too old for this running," Eric complained loudly.

In four minutes the trap was at the pier, hitched to a convenient light post.

"Here they come," said Eric excitedly.

Martha could see the *Mary* coming in. She frowned. "The ship isn't being handled with the usual verve. Maybe Matthew is sick."

"I don't think so. Perhaps Jarrell is handling the ship." Eric paused and then clarified, "As a matter of fact, I see your husband astern talking to Lieutenant Velasquez, and I don't think Jarrell is bringing the ship in either."

"Well, who is?" Martha asked rather anxiously.

"Some young fellow wearing a lieutenant's cap and a sailor's jacket. He's standing up on the bulwark in his bare feet. He probably left his shoes on the deck so he wouldn't scratch up the paint work."

Martha frowned. "He may be handling the ship, but he's not even using a speaking trumpet."

Then the young man looked forward and aft and gave orders to the helm, "Right full rudder!" Then he yelled to the boatswain, "Down all sails!"

The ship began to swing to starboard. The distance between the ship and the pier closed to about fifty yards and stayed there.

Eric said, "Just a little wide, but he's being careful with her."

Martha shrugged. "She looks all right to me."

The young lieutenant bellowed, "Get over one, two, and six lines."

Eric grinned, "He's got a good voice."

The young man was still at it, climbing back and forth along the top of the bulwark. "Get the fenders over! We don't want to scratch any of the paint work."

The young sailors, now trying to make one of their own look good, scurried after the fenders and lowered them between the ship's side and the piling.

"Move number two to the capstan! Smartly!" ordered Harrison.

The sailors did just that, and the strain was brought on number two line by the sailors walking around the capstan. Drops of sea water were squeezed out of the tautening line and the ship "walked alongside" slowly.

As the ship's side neared the pier, the fenders groaned as they were squeezed between the ship and the pier.

The captain walked over in a leisurely manner to the side, inspected the arrangements and results, and nodded to Lieutenant Harrison. "Good landing, Lieutenant. Now secure and double up the mooring lines."

Jarrell stood well back, grinning. His protegé had done a good job.

The crew trooped aft to hear Lieutenant Jarrell publish the first liberty list. There were both cheers and groans, and the first liberty group went below to get ready to leave the ship.

Martha looked eagerly at young Lieutenant Harrison. "Do you suppose he'll be ashore soon?" she asked Eric.

Eric laughed. "Certainly not. He'll be about four days down the list. He's the junior lieutenant."

———

Matthew came down the brow, resplendent in his captain's uniform, but Martha thought he was moving a little slowly. She turned to Eric. "Do you suppose he's been wounded?"

"He couldn't go forever without it happening. There is a

little damage to the ship. Let's just see how he gets into the trap."

He was a little slow, but Martha hoped it was just old age. He folded her in his arms, and his father reached out and clapped him on the back.

Martha was suspicious. "Are you sure you're all right?"

Matthew laughed. "Well, just a little bang-up on my right thigh. But I'm fine."

Martha frowned. "Let's go home. Eric, you stay here and take charge of the rest of the arrival."

Matthew insisted, "But, Martha, I'm all right."

"No, you aren't. Let's go. I'll send the trap back to pick up Eric."

All the way home the citizens waved at the Captain and his wife. Martha was anxious to get home, but Matthew drove slowly so he could return their waves.

He looked at her sideways. "You haven't asked me how we did. There's a prize frigate anchored out in the river and two more merchant prizes are headed for Portsmouth. I think we did very well."

Martha shook her head. "But you and your ship. I saw some damage to your ship, and I suspect you have more yourself than you've admitted."

"The damned commodore led us right into trouble, but we got out all right."

"You always do, but I still have a feeling you were quite close to disaster this time."

Chapter 36

As Eric's eager horses pulled the trap slowly up Church Street, Martha realized that Matthew was holding the horses down to a trot, and she looked inquiringly at him. "Do you hurt somewhere?"

Matthew grinned. "Just a little. I wanted to say hello to some of the passing citizens."

"I think you should forget about socializing now, unless you are thinking about becoming a politician some day. You need to get home and rest."

"It was very interesting to meet our Congressman and to get to know him more personally at dinner the other night."

"What did you think of him?" Martha asked.

Matthew shrugged. "He's a nice guy, but not too smart. He's reasonably honest."

"What do you mean by reasonably?"

"He takes money from us, but all Congressmen have to take some money. They can't live on their pay alone."

"What would you do in that position?"

"That's just it. I would be well off financially, and I could vote my conscience independently."

"Sounds interesting."

"I'll think about it. This country has given me a lot, and I'd like to do something for it."

"You're doing that right now by wearing the uniform and fighting for it. You should have a feeling of accomplishment."

Matthew shrugged. "Yes. That may be enough. We'll see."

As the trap neared the front entry, Matthew slowed the horses to a walk. When they reached the front door, Martha scampered down from her seat and tied the horses loosely to a hitching post. "I'll get Jebediah's younger son to take them back to Eric. The boy loves to drive them, and he's very careful."

Martha came aft to the folding stairs, pulled them down, and handed Matthew down.

They went up the stairs slowly, hand in hand. At the top Matthew regained his composure and in turn handed Martha through the door.

The maid was waiting inside, followed by the two cooks. Martha said, "We'll have a pre-lunch drink and after that a light lunch." Martha led her husband onto the glassed-in porch with the sun streaming in to warm it. They sat down side by side on a couch.

Martha, with a serious look in her eye, asked her husband, "Now, Matthew, what happened?"

"I can't hide it from you. I was wounded ten days ago. But now I've almost completely recovered."

"Maybe, but I want to look at the wound after lunch."

Matthew began a half-hour story about their cruise and the troubles he had had with the commodore. As he got nearer to the recounting of the battle, he got up and began to pace, snapping his fingers, obviously upset.

Martha shook her head slowly. "Please, Matthew, sit down beside me and take your time. You sound like this period of history is neither good nor bad."

"You mean what the historians are beginning to call the Quasi-War?"

Martha shrugged. "It's a real war as far as I'm concerned, even if it's not a legally declared war. I guess 'quasi' is a good description."

"Maybe so, but people still get killed and ships are still sunk. It's a full war as far as I'm concerned."

Matthew sipped his drink and then changed hands holding it and drained the glass. "The damned Frenchmen were bastards. I'm glad we beat them, legally or not. In any event we made millions of dollars at their expense. Five years ago our family fortunes had reached a new low. Now the company is once again solvent, and our family and its descendants are well provided for."

"Yes, you're right Matthew. Now I think we can go back to talking about politics.

You were apparently considering trying to be a congressman someday. I think you should give it a try. You'd make a fine one."

Matthew sighed. "If you agree I'll try it, but not right away." Matthew's leg was beginning to hurt him, so he eased into a heavily padded chair.

Martha, watching him carefully, said, "Let's go have lunch. You can tell me about the final battle tonight."

—————

Lunch was very good, but both were on edge. When it was over, Martha grinned, came around the table, and took Matthew's hand. "Time for a nap now, sailor. This will be your last nap as a sailor."

"What do you mean?" Matthew asked, puzzled.

"Eric was too busy to tell you. Tomorrow the Navy, as we know it, will be disbanded. You will once again be a merchant ship captain. That is, if you want to be. Your officers and your enlisted men are no longer in the Navy. The *Mary* is yours again, and you have a fleet of four merchantmen. You will have a flotilla of your own."

Matthew pondered this piece of news briefly before asking Martha, "Have you heard anything from Bruce?"

"Oh, yes. The *United States* is being laid up also. Bruce should be home on or before Christmas."

"And he's a civilian again?"

"Yes, so I suppose he can sail in your ships."

"Yes, I'll start him out on the *Mary* with Jarrell. Jebediah will be going back to his restaurant and Velasquez will be retiring."

"What about that young man with no need for a speaking trumpet, Harrison?"

"Jarrell will need him, too."

"You told me before you started on your last cruise you wanted to come home soon," Martha said hopefully.

"Very much. Like tomorrow, and for good."

"And your father?"

"He'll be busy at the shipyard converting the ships. When he's finished I think his wife will want him to come back to the horse farm. John Paul will take over running the shipyard for the family." Matthew stretched luxuriously. "You promised me a nap. Let's move to the bedroom."

Martha rose and said something to the maid. Then she took Matthew's hand and led him upstairs. When she had closed and locked the bedroom door, she said, "Well, old man, that means you have several months on your hands. You can try out the politics that we talked about."

"And you?"

"Not so much outside the house. I plan to be busy."

"How's that?"

"The doctor says I can safely have a sixth child."

"What! Do you really want one?"

"I certainly do. I've been trying to find a convenient time for years. You were always coming or going to sea. Now let's get your trousers off and see to your wound."

"Is the bedroom door locked?"

"Of course. Didn't you see me lock it? And the maid has strict orders not to bother us until dinner."

"Well, I don't think I've ever removed my trousers in the daytime in the presence of ladies."

"This will be a first time. Get to it, or I'll pull them off myself."

"And yours?"

"We'll see after I find out what kind of shape you're in."

The trousers came off. Like most sailors, Matthew wore no underclothes, and all of him was soon revealed with his well-turned legs, "Do I pass muster?" Matthew asked, grinning slyly at his wife.

"Yes. You look fine, but that wound was a close call. Now to find out how you perform."

Matthew smiled. "How about your trousers?"

Martha laughed. "You ought to know women don't

wear trousers. Come to bed if you want to find out what I wear in the daytime."